Preston sto ... **pajama pants,** ... **his waist and** ... **at his feet.**

His gaze met and fused with Chandra's as he stepped out of them. Her breath quickened and his erection pulsed when he noticed the outline of her hardened nipples against the white tank top.

He stared at her, wanting to commit to memory the cloud of dark hair around her face, breasts that were fuller than he'd expected and the look of indecision in the eyes staring back at him in anticipation.

The mattress dipped slightly when he placed one knee, then the other on the bed. Lying beside Chandra, Preston turned to face her. "How are you?"

A tentative smile trembled across her lips. "I'm good, Preston."

He ran the back of his hand over her cheek. "Are you ready for this? If not, then we can sleep together without making love."

Shifting slightly, Chandra draped her leg over his. "I'm ready."

Books by Rochelle Alers

Kimani Romance

Bittersweet Love
Sweet Deception
Sweet Dreams

ROCHELLE ALERS

has been hailed by readers and booksellers alike as one of today's most popular African-American authors of women's fiction. With nearly 2 million copies of her novels in print, Ms. Alers is a regular on the Waldenbooks, Borders and *Essence* bestseller lists, and has been the recipient of numerous awards, including a Gold Pen Award, an Emma Award, a Vivian Stephens Award for Excellence in Romance Writing, an *RT Book Reviews* Career Achievement Award and a Zora Neale Hurston Literary Award. A native New Yorker, Ms. Alers currently lives on Long Island. Visit her Web site at www.rochellealers.com.

Sweet Dreams

ROCHELLE ALERS

KIMANI
ROMANCE

Let him kiss me with the kisses of his mouth;
for thy love is better than wine.
—*The Song of Solomon* 1:2

 KIMANI PRESS™

Recycling programs
for this product may
not exist in your area.

ISBN-13: 978-0-373-86152-1

SWEET DREAMS

Dear Reader,

I would like to thank you for your enthusiastic response to the Eatons and their extended family. You were introduced to Belinda in *Bittersweet Love* and Myles in *Sweet Deception*. Now for those who want to revisit the Eatons I give you *Sweet Dreams*, the latest installment in the miniseries.

All of us dream, but do we remember them upon waking? Not only does Chandra Eaton remember her sexy dreams but she also writes them down. Then the unspeakable happens when she misplaces her journal and none other than Preston Tucker, Philadelphia's award-winning dramatist, finds and reads her erotic fantasies. They even become the plot for his latest play. More than sparks fly when she and Preston bring the dreams to life!

Look for Denise Eaton to take center stage in October 2010 when a former lover finds *Temptation at First Sight*.

Yours in romance,

Rochelle Alers

When she did move, it was to reach over and turn on

Prologue

The sound of labored breathing competed with the incessant whirring of the blades of the ceiling fan overhead. The crescendo of gasps and moans overlapped with the rhythmic thrum of the fan as it circulated the humid tropical night air coming through the screened-in jalousie windows.

It was a scene that had played out nightly countless times since Chandra Eaton had come to Belize to teach. Her right hand cupped her breast while the other fondled her mound, as she surrendered to the surging contractions rippling through her thighs. Arching her back, she exhaled as the last of the orgasm that had held her in the throes of an explosive climax left her feeling as if she'd been shattered into a million pieces.

She lay motionless, savoring the aftermath that made it almost impossible to move or draw a normal breath. When she did move, it was to reach over and turn on the lamp on the bedside table. The soft golden glow cast shadows over the sparsely decorated bedroom.

Biting her lip, Chandra sat upright and picked up the pen lying atop her cloth-covered journal. Unscrewing the top, she closed her eyes for several seconds. The tip of the pen was poised over a clean page before she sighed and collected her thoughts.

Dream #139—October 2
I could smell him, feel him, taste him, but as usual he wouldn't let me touch his face.

His hand feathered over my leg, moving up slowly until it rested along my inner thigh. My breathing quickened, filling the bedroom with hiccuping sounds. I was so aroused that I hadn't wanted prolonged foreplay. I'd screamed and pleaded for him to make it quick. His response was to place one hand over my mouth, while he used his free hand to guide his engorged erection inside me. The heat from his body, the rigid flesh moving in and out of my body made my heart stop beating for several seconds.

He was relentless, pushing and receding. And then, slowing just before I climaxed, I'd pleaded with him to make love to me and then I begged him to stop. I felt faint. But he didn't stop. And I let go, abandoning myself to the pleasure of a sweet, explosive orgasm. Instead of lying beside me on the mattress, he got up and left. It was as if he knew it would be our last time together.

Chandra reread what she'd written, and then smiled. It was uncanny the way she was able to remember her dreams with vivid clarity. They'd begun the first week she arrived in Belize, and had continued for more than two years. They didn't come every night. But when they did, they served to assuage the sexual tension that came from not sharing her body with a man in nearly three years.

The dreams came without warning. She had begun to see them as a release for her stress and frustration. She didn't know who the man was who came to her when she least expected it, and she didn't care as long as he provided the stimulation needed to give her the physical release so necessary for her sexual well-being.

Smiling, Chandra closed the journal, capped the pen, turned off the lamp and slid under the covers, lying on the pillow that cradled her head. Minutes later she closed her eyes. This time when she fell asleep, there were no erotic dreams to disturb her slumber.

Chapter 1

Chandra Eaton slumped against the rear seat in the taxi as the driver maneuvered away from the curb at the Philadelphia International Airport. She felt as if she'd been traveling for days. Her flight from Belize to Miami was a little more than two hours. But it was the layover in Atlanta that had lasted more than eight hours because of violent thunderstorms that left her out of sorts. All she wanted was a hot shower, a firm bed and a soft, fluffy pillow.

As a Peace Corps volunteer, she'd spent more than two years teaching in Belize. She'd returned to Philadelphia twice: once to attend the funeral of her eldest sister and brother-in-law, and three months ago to be a bridesmaid in the wedding of her surviving sister, Belinda. Now, at the age of thirty, she'd come home again. But this time it was to stay.

Her father called her his gypsy, and her mother said

she was a vagabond, to which she had no comeback. What no one in her family knew, her parents in particular, was that she'd been running away from the tragedy that had befallen one of her students, followed by her own broken engagement.

Thankfully, her previous homecoming and this one would be more joyful occasions. Belinda had married Griffin Rice in June and two months ago her brother Myles had exchanged vows with Zabrina Mixon-Cooper after a ten-year separation. She also looked forward to meeting her nephew for the first time.

"What the…"

She opened her eyes and sat up straighter, her heart slamming against her ribs. The cabbie had swerved to avoid hitting another vehicle drifting into their lane. Her purse and leather tote slid off the seat and onto the floor with the violent motion, spilling their contents. Bending over, she retrieved her cell phone, wallet, passport and a pack of mints. Then she checked the tote to make certain her laptop was still there.

"Are you all right back there, miss?" the driver asked over his shoulder.

Chandra exhaled audibly. "I'm good," she lied smoothly.

She wasn't good. If she'd been a cat, she would've used up at least one of her nine lives. It was going to be some time before she would be able to adjust to the fast pace of a large urban city. Living in Philadelphia, even in one of its suburbs, was very different from living and teaching in a small town in Northern Belize.

The cabdriver took a quick glance in the rearview mirror. "Let me try and get around this clown before I end up in his trunk."

Settling back again, Chandra closed her eyes. When

she'd called her mother to tell her that her flight had been delayed, Roberta Eaton had offered to drive to the airport to pick her up. But she'd told her mother she would take a taxi to the subdivision where her parents had purchased a two-bedroom, two-bath town house. Aside from her purse and tote bag, she had checked only one piece of luggage. The trunk with most of her clothes was scheduled to arrive in the States at the end of the month.

It appeared as if she'd just fallen asleep when the motion stopped, and she opened her eyes. Chandra missed the six-bedroom, four-bath farmhouse where she'd grown up with her sisters and brother. She understood her parents' need to downsize now that they were in their sixties. They didn't want to concern themselves with having someone shovel snow or mow the lawn, or deal with the exorbitant expense of maintaining a large house.

What she'd missed most was opening the door leading from the main house and into the connecting space that had been Dr. Dwight Eaton's medical practice. Her father didn't schedule patients between the hours of twelve and one; the exception was in an emergency. It had been her time to have her father all to herself. Gathering her purse and tote, she paid the fare, opened the rear door and stepped out of the taxi as the driver came around to retrieve her luggage from the trunk, setting it on the front steps.

Roberta Eaton stood in the entryway. The smile that parted her lips caused the skin around her eyes to crinkle. She prayed that this homecoming would be Chandra's last. She thought she knew all there was to know about her youngest child, but Chandra's mercurial moods kept her guessing as to what she would do or where she would go next.

What she'd found so off-putting was that there was usually no warning. It was if her daughter went to sleep, then woke with a new agenda, shocking everyone with her announcements. First it was her decision not to attend the University of Pennsylvania, but Columbia University in New York City. Then she'd declined an offer to teach at a Philadelphia elementary school and instead taught at a private all-girls' school in Northern Virginia. The most shocking, and what Roberta thought most devastating, was when Chandra announced she'd joined the Peace Corps and decided to teach in Belize. Although she'd become accustomed to her daughter's independent nature, it was her husband, Dwight Eaton, who said his youngest daughter had caused him many sleepless nights.

Roberta approached Chandra with outstretched arms, the tears she'd tried vainly to hold back overflowed. "Welcome home, baby."

Her mother calling her *baby* was Chandra's undoing. She could deal with any and everything except her mother's tears. Roberta was openly weeping—deep, heart-wrenching sobs that made Chandra unleash her own flood of tears.

Pressed closer to Roberta's ample bosom, she tightened her hold around her mother's neck, savoring the warmth of the protective embrace. "Mama, please don't cry."

Roberta's tears stopped as if she'd turned off a spigot. "Don't tell me not to cry when I've had too many sleepless nights and worn out my knees praying that you'd make it home safely."

Easing back, Chandra stared at her mother. Roberta

Eaton hadn't changed much over the years. Her body was fuller and rounder, and there was more salt than pepper in her short natural hairstyle. Her face had remained virtually unchanged. Her dark brown complexion was clear, her skin smooth.

"I'm home, Mama."

"You're home, but for how long, Chandra Eaton? I was talking to your father last night, and we have a wager that you won't hang around for more than three to six months before you start getting itchy feet again."

"I'm not going anywhere. I'm home to stay."

Roberta gave her a look that said *I don't believe you*, but Chandra was too tired to get into an argument with her mother. She'd been up since two that morning for a 5:00 a.m. flight to Miami, with a connecting flight to Atlanta. Sitting in Hartsdale for hours had tried her patience, and that meant she had no intention of engaging in a conversation where she had to defend herself or convince her mother that she didn't plan to leave home again. Once she'd completed her tour with the Peace Corps she'd promised herself that she would stop running away, that she would come home, face her fears and reconcile her past.

"May I please go into the house and shower before going to bed?"

As if she'd come out of a trance, Roberta leaned forward and kissed Chandra's cheek. Within seconds she'd morphed into maternal mode. "I'm sorry, baby. You have to be exhausted. Did you eat?" she asked over her shoulder as she stepped into the spacious entryway.

"I ate something at the airport."

Picking up her luggage, Chandra walked into the house and made her way toward the staircase to the second floor guest bedroom. Methodically, she stripped off her clothes, leaving them on the bathroom floor, and stepped into the shower stall. Her eyelids were drooping by the time she'd dried off. She searched through her luggage for a nightgown and crawled into bed. It was just after six. And even though the sun hadn't set, within minutes of her head touching the pillow she was asleep.

Preston Tucker ducked his head as he got into the taxi and gave the driver the address to his duplex in downtown Philadelphia. He'd spent the past twenty-four hours flying to Los Angeles for a meeting that lasted all of ten minutes before returning to Philadelphia after flying standby from LAX.

He'd told his agent that he had reservations about meeting with studio executives who wanted to turn one of his plays into a movie with several A-list actors. But all Clifford Jessup could see were dollar signs. Preston knew if he sold the movie rights to his play he would have to relinquish literary control. But he was unwilling to do so at the expense of not being able to recognize his play, something he'd spent more than two years writing and perfecting, breathing life into the characters.

He was aware of Hollywood's reputation for taking literary license once they'd optioned a work, but the suits he'd spoken to wanted to eviscerate his play. If he'd been a struggling playwright he probably would've accepted their offer. But fortunately for him, his days of waiting for a check so that he could pay back rent were behind him. What made the play even more personal is that it was the first play he'd written as a college student.

Slumping in the rear seat, he tried to stretch his long legs out to a more comfortable position under the seat in front of him. His right foot hit something. Reaching under the passenger seat, he pulled out a slim black ostrich-skin portfolio with the initials *CE* stamped on the front in gold lettering. Looking at the driver's hack license, he noticed the man's first and last names began with an *M,* so he concluded a passenger had left it in the taxi.

Preston debated whether to open it or give it to the taxi driver, who most likely would turn it in to Lost and Found or discard the contents and keep the expensive-looking portfolio for himself. He decided to unzip it and found a cloth-bound journal. Judging from the mauve color of the book, he knew it belonged to a woman.

His suspicions were confirmed when he saw the neat cursive writing on the inside front cover: "If found, please return to Chandra Eaton." What followed was a telephone number with a Philadelphia area code and an e-mail address. Reaching into the breast pocket of his suit jacket, he took out his cell phone to dial the number, but the first sentence on the first page caused him to go completely still.

Dream #9—March 3

I opened my eyes when I heard the soft creaking sound that told me someone had opened my bedroom door. Usually he came in through the window. I held my breath because I wasn't certain if it was him. But who else would it be? I didn't know whether to scream or reach under the bed for the flashlight I kept there in the event of a power failure. I decided not to move, hoping whoever had come would realize they were in the wrong room and then leave.

The seconds ticked off and I found myself counting slowly, beginning with one. By the time

I'd counted to forty-three, there was no sound, no movement. I reached under the bed for the flashlight and flicked it on. I was alone in the bedroom, the sound of the runaway beating of my heart echoing in my ears and the lingering scent of a man's cologne wafting in the humid tropical air coming in through the open windows. I recognized the scent. It was the same as the one I'd given Laurence for our first Christmas together. But, he's gone, exorcised, so why did I conjure him up?

Preston slipped the cell phone back into his pocket as he continued to read. He was so engrossed in what Chandra Eaton had written that he hadn't realized the taxi had stopped and his building doorman had opened the rear door.

"Welcome home, Mr. Tucker."

His head popped up and he smiled. "Thank you, Reynaldo."

Preston returned the journal to the leather case, paid the driver and then reached for his leather weekender on the seat next to him. He'd managed to read four of Chandra Eaton's journal entries, each one more sensual and erotic than the one before it. As a writer, he saw scenes in his head before putting them down on paper, and he was not only intrigued but fascinated by what Chandra Eaton had written.

Clutching his weekender, he entered the lobby of the luxury high-rise, which had replaced many of the grand Victorian-style mansions that once surrounded Rittenhouse Square. He'd purchased the top two floors in the newly constructed building on the advice of his financial planner, using it as a business write-off. His office, a media room, gourmet kitchen, formal living and dining rooms were set up for work and entertaining. The three bedrooms with en suite bathrooms on the upper floor were for out-of-town guests.

There had been a time when he'd entertained at his Brandywine Valley home, but as he matured he'd come to covet his privacy. Lately, he'd become somewhat of a recluse. If an event wasn't work-related, then he usually declined the invitation. His mother claimed he was getting old and crotchety, to which he replied that thirty-eight was hardly old and he wasn't crotchety, just particular as to how he spent his time and more importantly with whom.

Preston was exhausted and sleep-deprived from flying more than six thousand miles in twenty-four hours. His original plan was to shower and go directly to bed, but Chandra Eaton's erotic prose had revived him. He would finish reading the journal, then e-mail the owner to let her know he'd found it.

He didn't bother to stop at the concierge to retrieve his mail, and instead walked into the elevator and pressed the button for his floor. The elevator doors glided closed. The car rose smoothly and swiftly, stopping at the eighteenth floor. The doors opened again and he made his way down a carpeted hallway to his condo.

It was good to be home. If he'd completely trusted Cliff Jessup to represent his interests, he never would've flown to L.A. What bothered him about his agent was that they'd practically grown up together. Both had attended Princeton, pledged the same fraternity, and he'd been best man at Cliff's wedding. Something had changed. Preston wasn't certain whether he'd changed, or if Cliff had changed, or if they were just growing apart.

Inserting the cardkey into the slot to his duplex, Preston pushed open the door and was greeted with a rush of cool air. He'd adjusted the air-conditioning before he left, but apparently the drop in the temperature outside made it feel uncomfortably chilly. It was mid-October, and the forecasts predicted a colder and snowier than usual winter.

He dropped his bag on the floor near a table his interior decorator had purchased at an estate sale. It was made in India during the nineteenth century for wealthy Indians and Europeans. It was transported from India to Jamaica at the behest of a British colonist who'd owned one of the largest sugarcane plantations in the Caribbean. Not only was it the most extravagant piece of furniture in the condo, but Preston's favorite.

Emptying his pockets of loose change, he put the coins in a crystal dish on the table along with his credit card case and cardkey. Floor lamps illuminated the living room and the chandelier over the dining room table sparkled like tiny stars bathing the pale walls with a golden glow. Preston worked well in bright natural sunlight, so he'd had all of the lamps and light fixtures programmed to come on at different times of the day and night.

There was a time when he'd thought he had writer's block, since he found it very difficult to complete a project during the winter months. It was only when he'd reexamined his high school and college grades that he realized they were much higher in the spring semester than the fall. When he mentioned it to a friend who was a psychologist, she said he probably suffered from SAD, or seasonal affective disorder. Knowing this, he developed a habit of beginning work on a new script in early spring.

Walking past the staircase leading to the upper level, he entered the bathroom that led directly into his office. He undressed, brushed his teeth, leaving his clothes on a covered bench before stepping into the shower stall. The sharp spray of icy-cold water revived him before he adjusted the water temperature to lukewarm. Despite his jet lag, Preston was determined to stay awake long enough to read more of the journal.

He didn't know why, but he felt like a voyeur. But instead of peeking into Chandra Eaton's bedroom, he had read her most intimate thoughts. He smiled. Either she had a very fertile imagination, or an incredibly active sex life.

After wiping the moisture from his body with a thick, thirsty towel, he slipped into a pair of lounging pants and a white tee from a supply on a shelf in an alcove in the bathroom suite. Fifteen minutes later, Preston settled onto a chaise lounge in his office with a large mug of steaming black coffee and the cloth-covered journal. It was after two in the morning when he finally finished reading. His eyes were burning, but what he'd read had been too arousing for him to go to sleep.

Turning on the computer, he waited for it to boot up. He e-mailed Chandra Eaton to inform her that he'd found her portfolio in a taxi and where she could contact him to retrieve it.

Chapter 2

Chandra opened one eye, then the other, peeking at the clock on the bedside table. It was after nine. She couldn't believe she'd been asleep for more than twelve hours. It was apparent she was more exhausted than she'd originally thought. And there was no doubt her body's time clock was off. If she were still in Belize she would've been in the classroom with her young students.

Stretching her arms above her head, she exhaled a lungful of air. Chandra was glad to be home and looked forward to reuniting with her family. Sitting up, she swung her legs over the side of the twin bed and walked into the bathroom. She had a laundry list of things to do before the weekend: get a complete beauty makeover—including a haircut, mani/pedi and a hydrating facial. Despite using the strongest sunblock and wearing a hat to protect her face, the rays of the Caribbean sun had dried out her skin. She also had to go online to search for public schools in the Philadelphia area. It was too late to be assigned a full-time teaching job, but she could find work as a substitute teacher. Her sister, Belinda, who'd moved to Paoli after she married Griffin Rice, still taught American history in one of the city's most challenging high schools.

After a leisurely shower, Chandra left the bathroom to prepare for her day. It felt good not to have to shower within the mandatory three-minute time limit, to avoid using up the hot water for the next person. She'd gotten used to taking short, and sometimes cold, showers. But it wasn't just soaking in a bathtub that made her aware of what she'd had to sacrifice when she'd signed up for the Peace Corps.

Her cousin Denise had offered to sublet her co-op to Chandra after she relocated to Washington, D.C. to accept a position as executive director of a child care center. Purchasing furniture for the co-op was another item on Chandra's to-do list. But her list and everything on it would have to wait until she had something to eat. She knew she wouldn't get to see her father, who had patients booked, until later that evening. Her mother divided her time between volunteering several days a week at a senior facility and quilting with several of her friends. The quartet of quilters had completed many projects for homebound and chronically ill children.

It was after eleven when Chandra returned to the bedroom to make the bed and clean up the bathroom. Bright autumn sunlight came in through the blinds when she sat down at the corner desk and opened her laptop. When she went online she saw e-mails from her sister, brother and her cousin Denise. Without reading them, she knew they were welcoming her home. There was another e-mail with an unfamiliar address and the subject: Lost and Found, that piqued her interest. She clicked on it:

Ms. Eaton,
I found your portfolio in a taxi. Please contact me at the following number to arrange for its return.
P. J. Tucker

Chandra stared at the e-mail, thinking it was either a hoax or spam. But how would the person know her name? And what portfolio was he referring to? She picked up her tote bag, searching through it thoroughly. The leather case her brother had given her as a gift for her college graduation wasn't there.

"No!" she hissed.

P. J. Tucker must have found her journal. It had to have fallen out when the taxi driver swerved to avoid hitting another vehicle. The journal was the first volume of three others she'd filled with accounts of her dreams. She was certain she'd packed all of them in the trunk until she found one in a drawer under her lingerie. Mister or Miss P. J. Tucker had to open the journal to find out where to contact her. Chandra prayed that was all he or she had looked at. The reason she'd put the journals in the trunk, which was stowed on a ship several days before she left Belize, was that she hadn't wanted custom agents to read it when they went through her luggage.

Reaching for her cell, she dialed the number in the e-mail. "May I please speak to Mister or Miss P. J. Tucker," she said when a deep male voice answered.

"This is P. J. Tucker."

Please don't tell me you read my journal, she prayed. "I'm Chandra Eaton."

"Ms. Eaton. No doubt you read my e-mail."

"Yes, and I'd like to thank you for finding my portfolio."

"It's a very nice case, Ms. Eaton. Is it ostrich skin?"

Chandra chewed her lip. It was apparent P. J. Tucker wanted to talk about something other than the material her portfolio was made from. She wanted to set up a time and place, so that she could retrieve her journal.

"Yes, Mr. Tucker, it is. I'd like to pick up my portfolio from you. But of course, whenever it's convenient for you."

"I'm free now if you'd like to come and pick it up."

"Where are you?" Reaching for a pen, Chandra wrote down the address. "How long are you going to be there?"

"All day and all night."

She smiled. "Well, I don't have all day or all night. What if I come by before noon?"

"I'll be here."

Her smile grew wider. "Goodbye."

"Later."

Chandra ended the call. She punched speed dial for a taxi, then quickly changed out of her shorts and T-shirt and into a pair of jeans that she paired with a white men's-tailored shirt, navy blazer and imported slip-ons. There wasn't much she could do with her hair, so she brushed it off her face, braided it and secured the end with an elastic band. She heard the taxi horn as she descended the staircase. Racing into the kitchen, she took the extra set of keys off a hook, leaving through the side door.

The address P. J. Tucker had given Chandra was a modern luxury condominium in the historic Rittenhouse neighborhood. One of her favorite things to do as a young girl was to accompany her siblings when their parents took them on Sunday-afternoon walking tours of Philadelphia neighborhoods, of which Rittenhouse was her personal favorite. It had been an enclave of upper-crust, Main Line, well-to-do families.

Dwight and Roberta Eaton always made extra time when they walked through Rittenhouse, lingering at the square honoring the colonial clockmaker, David Rittenhouse. Her father knew he had to be up on his history whenever Belinda asked questions about who'd designed the Victorian mansions, the names of the wealthy families who lived there and their contribution to the growth of the City of Brotherly Love.

Unlike her history-buff sister, Chandra never concerned herself with the past but with the here and now. She was too impulsive to worry about where she'd come from. It was where she was going that was her focus.

She paid the fare, stepped out of the taxi and walked into the lobby with Tiffany-style lamps and a quartet of cordovan-brown leather love seats. Although the noonday temperature registered sixty-two degrees, Chandra felt a slight chill. In Belize she awoke to a spectacular natural setting, eighty-degree temperatures, the sounds of colorful birds calling out to one another and the sweet aroma of blooming flowers, which made the hardships tolerable.

The liveried doorman touched the brim of his shiny cap. "Good afternoon."

Chandra smiled at the tall, slender man with translucent skin and pale blue eyes that reminded her of images she'd seen of vampires. The name tag pinned to his charcoal-gray greatcoat read Michael.

"Good afternoon. Mr. Tucker is expecting me."

"I'll ring Mr. Tucker to see whether he's in. Your name?"

"It's Miss Eaton."

Michael typed her name into the telephone console on a shelf behind a podium. Then he tapped in Preston Tucker's apartment number. Seconds later *ACCEPT* appeared on the display. His head came up. "Mr. Tucker will see you, Miss Eaton. He's in 1801. The elevators are on the left."

Chandra walked past the concierge desk to a bank of elevators, entered one and pushed the button for the eighteenth floor. The doors closed as the elevator car rose smoothly, silently to the designated floor. When the doors opened she found herself staring up at a man with skin reminiscent of gold-brown toffee. There was something about his face that seemed very familiar, and she searched her memory to figure out where she'd seen him before.

A hint of a smile played at the corners of his generous mouth. "Miss Eaton?"

She stepped out of the car, smiling. "Yes," she answered, staring at the proffered hand.

"Preston Tucker."

Chandra's jaw dropped. She stared dumbfounded, looking at the award-winning playwright whose critically acclaimed dramas were mentioned in the same breath as those of August Wilson, Eugene O'Neill and Tennessee Williams. She'd just graduated from college when he had been honored by the mayor of New York and earned the New York Drama Critics' Circle Award for best play of the year. At the time, he'd just celebrated his thirtieth birthday and it was his first Broadway production.

Preston Tucker wasn't handsome in the traditional

way, although she found him quite attractive. He towered over her five-four height by at least ten inches and the short-sleeved white shirt, open at the collar, and faded jeans failed to conceal the power in his lean, muscular physique. Her gaze moved up, lingering on a pair of slanting, heavy-lidded, sensual dark brown eyes. There was a bump on the bridge of his nose, indicating that it had been broken. It was his mouth, with a little tuft of hair under his lower lip, and cropped salt-and-pepper hair that drew her rapt attention. She doubted he was forty, despite the abundance of gray hair.

She blinked as if coming out of a trance and shook his hand. "Chandra Eaton."

Preston applied the slightest pressure on her delicate hand before releasing her fingers. Chandra Eaton was as sensual as her writings. She possessed an understated sexiness that most women had to work most of their lives to perfect. He stared at her almond-shaped eyes, high cheekbones, pert nose and lush mouth. Flyaway wisps had escaped the single plait to frame her sun-browned round face.

"Please come with me, Miss Eaton, and I'll get your portfolio." Turning on his heels, he walked the short distance to his apartment, leaving her to follow.

Chandra found herself staring for the second time within a matter of minutes when she walked into the duplex with sixteen-foot ceilings and a winding staircase leading to a second floor. Floor-to-ceiling windows brought in sunlight, offering panoramic views of the city. The soft strains of classical music floated around her from concealed speakers.

Her gaze shifted to the magnificent table in the foyer. "Oh, my word," she whispered.

Preston stopped and turned around. "What's the matter?"

Reaching out, Chandra ran her fingertips over the surface of the table. "This table. It's beautiful."

"I like it."

"You like it?"

"Yes, I do," he confirmed.

"I'd thought you'd say that you love it, and because you didn't I'm going to ask if you're willing to sell it, Mr. Tucker?"

"Preston," he corrected. "Please call me Preston."

"I'll call you Preston, but only if you stop referring to me as Miss Eaton."

His eyebrows lifted. "What if I call you Chandra?"

She smiled. "That'll do. Now, back to my question, *Preston*. Are you willing to sell the table?"

He smiled, the gesture transforming his expression from solemn to sensual. "Chandra," he repeated. "Did you know that your name is Sanskrit for *of the moon?*"

"No, I didn't." A slight frown marred her face. "Why do I get the feeling you're avoiding my question?"

Preston reached for her hand, leading her into the living room and settling her on a sand-colored suede love seat. He sat opposite her on a matching sofa.

"I'd thought you'd get the hint that I don't want to sell it."

Her frown deepened. "I don't do well with hints, Preston. All you had to say was no."

"*No* is not a particularly nice word, Chandra."

She wrinkled her nose, unaware of the charming quality of the gesture. "I'm a big girl, and that means I can deal with rejection."

Resting his elbows on his knees, Preston leaned in

closer. "If that's the case, then the answer is no, no and no."

Chandra winked at him. "I get your point." She angled her head while listening to the music filling the room. "Isn't that *Cavalleria Rusticana*—Intermezzo from *Godfather III?*"

An expression of complete shock froze Preston's face. He hadn't spent more than five minutes with Chandra Eaton and she'd surprised him not once but twice. She'd recognized the exquisite quality of the Anglo-Indian table and correctly identified a classical composition.

"Yes, it is. Are you familiar with Pietro Mascagni's work?"

"He's one of my favorites."

Preston gestured to the gleaming black concert piano several feet away. "Do you play?"

"I haven't in a while," Chandra admitted half-truthfully. She had played nursery rhymes and other childish ditties for her young students on an out-of-tune piano that had been donated to the school by a local church in Belize. Some of the keys didn't work, but the children didn't seem to notice when they sang along and sometimes danced whenever she played an upbeat, lively tune.

"Do you have any other favorites?" Preston asked.

"Liszt, Vivaldi and Dvorak, to name a few."

"Ah, the Romantics."

"What's wrong with being a Romantic?" Chandra knew she came off sounding defensive, yet she was past caring. As soon as she retrieved her things, she would be on her way.

"Nothing."

"If it's nothing, then why did you make it sound like a bad thing?" she asked.

"It's not a bad thing, Chandra. It's just that I'm not a romantic kind of guy," Preston countered with a wink.

She felt a shiver of annoyance snake its way up her spine. "Anyone can tell that if they've read or seen your plays. They're all dark, brooding and filled with pathos."

Preston realized Chandra Eaton had him at a disadvantage. She knew about him and he knew nothing about her, except what she'd written in her journal. And, he wasn't certain whether she'd actually experienced what she'd written or if it was simply a fantasy.

"That's because I'm dark *and* brooding."

"Being sexy and brooding works if you're a vampire," Chandra shot back.

"You like vampires?"

"Yes. But only if they are sexy."

"I thought all vampires were sexy, given their cinematic popularity nowadays."

"Not all of them," she said.

"What would make a vampire sexy, Chandra?"

"He would have to be…" Her words trailed off. She threw up a hand. "What am I doing? Why am I telling you things you probably already know?"

"You're wrong, Chandra. I don't know. Perhaps you can explain what the big fuss is all about."

She stared, speechless. "Are you blowing smoke, or do you really want to know?"

Quickly rising from the sofa and going down on one knee, Preston grasped her hand, tightening his grip when she tried to pull free. "I'm begging you, Chandra Eaton. I need your help." He was hard-pressed not to laugh when Chandra stared at him with genuine concern in her eyes. He didn't need her help with character development as much as he wanted to know what motivated her to write about her dreams.

"You're serious about this, Preston?"

"Of course I'm serious."

"Get up, Preston."

"What?"

"Get up off your knees. You look ridiculous."

"I thought I was being noble."

"Get up!"

"Yes, ma'am." Preston came to his feet and sat down again.

Chandra rolled her eyes at him. "I'm not old enough to be a ma'am."

"How old do you have to be?"

"At least forty," she said.

"Don't worry, I'm not going to ask your age."

"It's not a deep, dark secret," she said, smiling. "I'm thirty."

"You're still a kid."

"I stopped being a kid a long time ago. Now, back to my helping you develop a sexy character. What are you going to do with the information?"

"Maybe I'll write a play about two star-crossed lovers."

"That's already been done. *Romeo and Juliet, Love Story* and *West Side Story*."

"Has it been done on stage as a musical with vampires and mortals?"

Unexpected warmth surged through Chandra as her gaze met and fused with Preston Tucker's. She didn't want to believe she was sitting in his living room, talking to the brilliant playwright.

"But you don't write musicals."

"There's always a first time. It could be like *Phantom of the Opera,* or *Evita.*"

"Where would it be set?"

Closing his eyes, Preston stroked the hair under his lower lip. "New Orleans." When he opened his eyes they were shimmering with excitement. "The early nineteenth-century French Quarter rife with voodoo, prostitution, gambling and opium dens and beautiful quadroons with dreams of becoming *plaçées* in *marriages de la main gauche.*"

Chandra pressed her palms together at the same time she compressed her lips. How, she thought, had he come up with a story line so quickly? Now she knew why he'd been awarded a MacArthur genius grant. The plot was dark, but with a cast of sexy characters and the mysterious lush locale, there was no doubt the play would become a sensation.

"Would you also write the music?" she asked Preston.

"No. I know someone who would come up with what I want for the music and lyrics."

"What about costumes?"

"What about them, Chandra?"

"Women's attire changed from antebellum-era ball gowns to the flowing diaphanous dresses of the Regency period. Are your characters going to be demure, or will they favor scandalous décolletage?"

Staring at the toes of his slip-ons, Preston pondered her question. "I'd like to believe the folks in the French Quarter didn't always conform to the societal customs of the day. Remember, we're talking about naughty *Nawlins.*"

"It sounds as if it's going to be just a tad bit wicked."

When she smiled, an elusive dimple in her left cheek winked at him.

"Just a tad," he confirmed. "When do you think we can get together to talk about developing a sexy vampire story?"

Chandra narrowed her eyes at Preston. Was he, she thought, blowing smoke, or was he actually serious about needing her input? "I'll be in touch." She wasn't going to commit until she gave his suggestion more thought.

"You'll be in touch," Preston repeated. "When? How?" Chandra stood up, as did Preston.

"I have your e-mail address, so whenever I clear my calendar I'll e-mail you."

The seconds ticked as they stared at each other. "Okay. Let me go and get your portfolio."

Walking over to the window, Chandra stood and stared down at the street. She couldn't wait to tell her cousin Denise that she'd met Preston Tucker. After graduating from college, she and Denise had regularly traveled to New York to see Broadway plays. Every third trip they would check into a New York City hotel and spend the night. A few times they were able to convince their dates to accompany them, which worked out well since the guys always wanted to hang out at jazz clubs in and around Manhattan.

She turned when she heard footsteps. Preston had returned with her portfolio and handed it to her. Myles had given it to her along with a lesson plan book for her college graduation, and she had continued to use it while in Belize.

"Thank you for taking care of this for me," she said. Chandra valued Myles's gift as much as she did the contents of her journal.

Preston cupped her elbow and escorted her to the door. "I'll see you downstairs."

She gave him a sidelong glance. "I think I can make it downstairs all right."

"I'll still go down with you, because I need to pick up my mail."

Chandra and Preston rode the elevator in silence, parting in the lobby. She felt the heat from his gaze boring into her as she walked out into the bright autumn sunlight. She strolled along a street until she found a café with outdoor seating.

She ordered a salad Nicoise and a glass of white zinfandel and then called her cousin at the child care center. It rang three times before her voice mail switched on. "Denise, Chandra. Call me back tonight when you get home. I just met your idol. Later."

She ended the call, smiling. If anyone knew anything at all about Preston Tucker, it was Denise Eaton. Chandra decided she would wait until she heard from her cousin before she agreed to meet Preston again.

Chapter 3

Preston silently chastised himself for forgetting his manners. He hadn't offered Chandra Eaton anything to eat or drink. It was apparent that his annoyance with his agent sending him on a six-thousand-mile wild-goose chase had affected him more than he wanted to admit. If Clifford had been in the room with him during the negotiations, there was no doubt he would've fired the man on the spot. Wanting to avoid a fight, he decided to wait, wait until Clifford contacted him.

He retrieved his mail and then returned to the apartment. A smile tilted the corners of his mouth when he recalled his conversation with the young woman who'd recorded dreams so erotic, so sensual that he felt as if he'd actually entered the dream and it was he who'd made love to Chandra. He'd taken one shower, then hours later he was forced to take another one. Standing under the spray of ice-cold water was the antidote to an erection that had him thinking of doing what he hadn't done since adolescence.

Preston hadn't lied to Chandra when he told her he wasn't romantic in the true sense of the word. Yet he'd never mistreated or cheated on any woman he was seeing. He'd grown up witnessing his father passively and aggressively abuse his mother until she'd become an emotional cripple. Craig Tucker had never raised his voice or hit him or his sister, Yolanda. But whenever he drank to an excess, he blamed his wife for his failures, of which there were a few. A two-pack-a-day cigarette habit and heavy drinking took its toll, and Craig suffered a massive coronary at forty.

Walking into his home office, Preston put the pile of letters and magazines on his desk. The idea of writing a dramatic musical was scary *and* exciting. And, although he'd mentioned using a vampire as a leading character, the truth was he knew nothing about them. Sitting in a leather chair, he reached for a pencil and a legal pad and began jotting down key words.

The sun had slipped lower in the sky, and long and short shadows filled the room when he finally glanced up at the clock on a side table. It was after five. He'd spent more than four hours outlining scenes for his untitled musical drama. What kept creeping into his head were the accounts of the dreams he'd read the night before.

A knowing smile softened the angles in his face. He suddenly had an idea for a plot.

Chandra spied her father's car when the taxi driver maneuvered into the driveway. She hadn't expected her father to come home so early. She paid the fare, and clutching the case to her chest, got out and walked to the door. It opened before she could insert her key into the lock.

She didn't have time to react before her father held her in a bear hug, lifting her off her feet. Wrapping her arms around his neck, she kissed his cheek. "Daddy, stop! You're crushing my ribs."

Dwight set his daughter on her feet. "I'm sorry about that, baby girl."

Chandra smiled at the man against whom she measured every man she'd met in her life. Her father was soft-spoken, patient and benevolent—and that was with his patients. He was all that and then some to his children. He'd always been supportive, telling them they could do or be anything they wanted to be.

It was her father she'd gone to when she contemplated going into the Peace Corps. He encouraged her to follow her dream *and* her heart, while Roberta had taken to her bed, all the while complaining that her youngest was going to be the death of her.

She smiled at her father. He looked the same at sixty-three as he had at fifty-three. His dark face was virtually wrinkle-free and his deep-set brown eyes behind a pair of rimless glasses reminded her of chocolate chips. His thinning cropped hair was now completely gray.

"What are you doing home so early, Daddy?"

Dwight tugged at the thick braid falling midway down his daughter's back. "My last two patients canceled, so I thought I'd come home early and take my favorite girls out to dinner."

"Do you mind if we postpone it to another time?"

Eyes narrowing, Dwight led Chandra into the entryway. He cradled her face between his palms. "Aren't you feeling well?"

"I'm well. It's just that I stopped to eat a little while

ago. I'm certain Mama would appreciate you taking her to a restaurant with dining and dancing."

"You know your mother was quite the dancer in her day."

"She still is," Chandra said. Roberta had danced nonstop at Belinda and Griffin's wedding. She kissed her father's cheek. "I have to go online and look for a job."

"I thought you were going to take some time off before you go back to teaching."

"I'd really like to, Daddy, but I have to buy some furniture before I move into Denise's co-op."

"You should talk to Belinda before you buy anything. She told your mother that she has a buyer for her house, and expects to close on it before Halloween."

Myles had stayed in Belinda's house during the summer, and then returned to Pittsburgh where he taught constitutional law at Duquesne University School of Law. Despite the uncertainty in the real estate market, Belinda was fortunate enough to find a buyer for her house.

Chandra couldn't see herself purchasing property at this time in her life. Although she'd told her parents she hadn't planned to live overseas again, she still wasn't certain of her future.

"I'll call her later," she said to her father. "You and Mama have fun, and if you two can't be good, then be careful," she teased.

He chuckled and was still chuckling as she climbed the staircase. She walked into her bedroom, slipped out of her shoes and blazer and then sat down at the desk. Turning on her laptop, Chandra searched the Philadelphia public schools Web site for openings. Surprisingly, she found ten—eight of which were in less-than-desirable neighborhoods. Her heart rate kicked into high gear. Instead of substituting she would apply for a full-time position. The one school that advertised for a Pre-K, third and fifth grade teacher was about a mile from Denise's co-op and close to Penn's Landing and to public transportation.

Chandra was so engrossed in copying down the names of the schools, their addresses and principals that she almost didn't hear her cell phone. She retrieved it from her handbag, glancing at the display. "Hello, cousin."

"Hello, yourself. When did you get back?"

"Yesterday. I called you because I had the pleasure of meeting Preston Tucker today." She held the phone away from her ear when a piercing scream came through the earpiece. "Denise! Calm down."

"You've got to tell me everything, and I do mean everything, Chandra."

Settling down on the bed, she told her cousin about leaving her portfolio in the taxi and Preston e-mailing her to let her know he'd found it. She was forthcoming, leaving nothing out when she related the conversation between her and the playwright, including that he wanted her to work with him to develop a vampirelike character for a new play.

"Are you going to do it?" Denise asked, her sultry contralto dropping an octave.

"That's why I called you. What do you know about him?"

"He's brilliant, but you probably know that. And he's never been married. There were rumors a little while back that he was engaged to marry an actress. But the tabloids said she ended it. He rarely gives interviews and manages to stay out of the spotlight. I've seen every one of his plays, and if I were given the chance to work with him, I'd jump at it."

"I'm flattered that he asked for my help, but why, Denise? Why me?"

"Maybe he likes you."

Chandra shook her head.

"I don't think so."

"What did you say to him?"

"What are you talking about, Denise?"

"You had to say something to Preston for him to ask you to develop a character for his next play."

A beat passed. "I told him that all his plays were dark and brooding, and he admitted that he was dark and brooding. I suppose when I said brooding works if he were a vampire, he took it as a challenge."

"There you go, Chandra. You just said the operative word—*challenge*. Preston Tucker's bound to have an ego as large as the Liberty Bell, so he expects you to put your money where your mouth is."

"It's either that or…"

"Or what?" Denise asked when she didn't finish her statement.

"Nothing."

Chandra had said nothing, although there was the possibility that Preston had read her journal. He hadn't mentioned that he'd read it, and she didn't want to ask because she didn't want to know if he had. The only way she would be able to find out was to work with him.

"I'm going to do it, Denise. I'm going to help the very talented P. J. Tucker develop a vampire character for his next play."

"Hot damn! My cousin's going to be famous."

"Yeah, right," Chandra drawled. "I'll let you know how it turns out."

"You better," Denise threatened. "I'd love to chat longer, but I have a board meeting in ten minutes."

"Are you coming up to Paoli this weekend?"

"I plan on being there. I'll see you in a couple of days. Later."

"Later," Chandra repeated before she ended the call.

She sat, staring at the sheers billowing in the cool breeze coming through the open windows. To say she was intrigued by Preston Tucker was an understatement. Something told her that he didn't need her or anyone's help with character development. Did he, as Denise claimed, like her?

Chandra shook her head as if to banish the notion. She knew she hadn't given off vibes that said she was interested in him. After her yearlong liaison with Laurence Breslin she had sworn off men. Whenever she affected what could best be described as a "screw face" most men kept their distance. The persistent ones were greeted with, "I'm not interested in men," leaving them to ponder whether she didn't like them or she was only interested in a same-sex liaison. She liked men—a lot. It was just that she wasn't willing to set herself up for more heartbreak.

She went back to the task of researching schools. All she had to do was update her résumé and submit the applications online. Flicking on the desk lamp, she scrolled through her old e-mails until she found the one from Preston, her fingers racing over the keys:

Hi Preston,
I'm available to meet with you Friday. Please call or e-mail to confirm.—CE

She didn't have to wait for a response when his AIM popped up on the upper left corner of the screen.

PJT: Hi CE. Friday is good with me. What time should I pick you up?

CE: You don't have to pick me up. I'll take a taxi to your place.

PJT: No, CE. You tend to lose things in taxis.

CE: You didn't have to go there.

PJT: Sorry.

CE: Apology accepted.

PJT: Will call tomorrow to let you know when driver will pick you up.

CE: O.K. I'll see you Friday. Meanwhile, think of a name for your vampire.

PJT: He's not my vampire, but yours. So, you do the honor.

CE: O.K. Good night.

PJT: Good night.

Chandra logged off. She mentally checked off what she had to do before meeting with Preston. She still had to unpack, call her sister Belinda and update her résumé. During lunch she'd called the salon and was given an appointment for Thursday at eleven. The Eatons had planned a get-together at Belinda and Griffin's for Saturday to celebrate Sabrina's and Layla's thirteenth birthday. She wasn't certain what her nieces wanted or needed, but decided to give them gift cards. Then, there was her ten-year-old nephew whom she would meet for the first time. Aunt Chandra would have to buy him something, too.

Chandra waited for the driver to come around and open the rear door for her. As promised, Preston had arranged for a driver to bring her to his apartment building. He'd also arranged for them to have brunch.

She gave the doorman her name and three minutes later she came face-to-face with Preston Tucker for the second time when the doors to the elevator opened.

Preston stared, completely surprised. He almost didn't recognize Chandra. She'd changed her hair. The braid was gone, replaced by a sleek style that framed her face and floated over her shoulders. It made her look older, more sophisticated.

"You look very nice."

Chandra couldn't stop the pinpoints of heat pricking her face. She'd lightly applied a little makeup and changed outfits twice before deciding on a tailored charcoal-gray pantsuit, white silk blouse and black patent leather pumps.

"Thank you."

Preston not only looked good, she thought, but he also smelled good. He wore a pair of black slacks and matching shirt and the stubble on his chin gave him a slightly roguish look. He'd admitted to being dark and brooding and his somber attire affirmed that. She didn't have to go very far to find the inspiration for her vampire. Preston Tucker was the perfect character.

"Have you come up with a name for your vampire?" Preston asked as he led Chandra down the hallway and into his apartment.

"I have," she admitted.

He closed the door and turned to stare at her. "What is it?"

"Pascual."

Preston angled his head. "Pascual or Paschal?"

"Pascual. It's Spanish and Hebrew for *Passover*. The name is somewhat exotic and implies that he's passed through a portal from another world to ours."

"If the setting is New Orleans, shouldn't you give him a French name?"

Chandra drew in a breath, held it and then let it out slowly. They hadn't even begun to work together and already he was questioning her. "I thought you said Pascual is *my vampire*."

"He is, Chandra."

"Then, please let me develop him the way I want, Preston. And that includes giving him a name that's Spanish. Remember, France lost control of New Orleans to Spain, then regained it before it was sold to the U.S."

Preston looked sheepish. "Unfortunately, history and languages weren't my best subjects."

"I have you at a disadvantage because my sister teaches American history to high school students."

"What do you teach?"

"How do you know I'm a teacher?"

Reaching for her hand, he gave her fingers a gentle squeeze. "Today you look and sound like a teacher. Besides, you didn't deny it. By the way, are you on sabbatical or are you playing hooky?"

Chandra's lips twitched as she tried not to smile. She

knew she had to remain alert with Preston. He probably processed everything she said within seconds. "I'm in between jobs."

"Come with me to the kitchen. We can talk while I cook."

Her eyebrows lifted. "You write, direct and cook. I'm impressed. What other talents are you hiding?"

Throwing back his head, Preston let loose genuine laughter. He'd found Chandra Eaton cute and very talented. What he hadn't counted on was that she could make him laugh.

"I don't know. You'll have to tell me."

"Maybe I should ask your girlfriend."

Preston's expression changed suddenly. He glared at her under hooded lids. "I don't have a girlfriend."

"What about a wife?" Chandra asked. Denise had said Preston was a bachelor, but she needed him to confirm his marital status.

"I also don't have a wife."

"Is it because you're not romantic?" Chandra asked, knowing she was treading into dangerous territory. She really didn't want to know any more about Preston than what Denise had told her. Whatever she would share with him was to be strictly business.

"Not being romantic has nothing to do with whether I'm married or involved with a woman."

"Are you a misogynist?"

"Of course not."

"Don't look so put out, Preston. I've read about a lot of high-profile men who date women, but detest them behind closed doors."

"Well, I'm not one of those down-low brothers." He hadn't lied to Chandra. It had taken many years and countless therapy sessions for him to let go of the enmity between he and his father. "Women should be loved and protected, not physically or emotionally abused."

"Spoken like a true romantic hero."

"Give it up, Chandra. It's not going to work."

"What's not going to work?"

"You're not going to turn me into a romantic hero."

She wrinkled her nose in a gesture Preston had come to appreciate. "You think not, Preston?"

"I know not, Chandra."

"We'll see," she drawled.

His eyes narrowed. "What are you hatching in that very cute head of yours?"

Chandra ignored his referring to her being cute. "Wait until I develop Pascual's character and you're forced to breathe life into what will become a vampire who's not only sexy but very romantic. You'll be the one who has to come up with the dialogue whenever he interacts with his romantic lead."

"We'll see," Preston said.

"Have you thought of a name for your new play?"

Taking a step, he dropped Chandra's hand, pulling her to his chest. Lowering his head and fastening his mouth to the column of her scented neck, Preston pressed a kiss there. He increased the pressure, baring his teeth and stopping short of nipping the delicate flesh.

"Death's Kiss," he whispered in her ear.

Chandra turned her head, her mouth inches from Preston's, breathing in his warm, moist breath. "You can't kill your heroine, Preston." Her gaze caressed the outline of his mouth seconds before he kissed her cheek.

"We'll see, won't we?" he said, smiling.

"What would I have to do to convince you to include a happy ending?"

"I'll think of something."

Bracing her hands against Preston's chest, Chandra sought to put some distance between them. "I don't like the sound of that."

Preston winked at her. "Not to worry, Chandra. You're safe with me."

Chandra recoiled when his words hit her like a stinging slap. "The last man I was involved with said the very same words to me. But in the end I was left to fend for myself. Thanks, but no thanks, Preston. I can take care of myself."

"Was he your husband?"

"No. Thank goodness we didn't get that far. But we were engaged."

"Do you want to talk about it?"

"No. Not because I don't want to. It's just that I can't."

Preston dropped a kiss on her fragrant hair. "Then you don't have to. Are you ready to eat?" he asked, changing the subject.

"What's on the menu for brunch?"

Resting a hand at the small of her back, he escorted Chandra toward the kitchen. "You have a choice of fresh fruit, pancakes, waffles, an omelet or bacon, sausage, ham and grits. To drink, there's herbal tea, regular and hazelnut coffee, orange, grapefruit or cranberry juice. As for cocktails you have a choice between a Bloody Mary and a mimosa."

"I prefer a mimosa." Chandra flashed an attractive pout. "I'm really impressed with you, Preston. I've never hung out with a guy who could cook."

Preston gave Chandra a sidelong glance, his gaze lingering on the tumble of hair falling around her face.

"I'm no Bobby Flay or Chef Jeff, but I can promise you won't come down with ptomaine poisoning."

"I think I'm going to enjoy working with you."

And I promise not to like you too much, she added silently.

It was what Chandra told herself every time she met a man to whom she felt herself attracted. It'd worked in the past and she was certain it would work with Preston Tucker.

Chapter 4

Chandra followed Preston into an expansive state-of-the art stainless-steel-and-black gourmet kitchen outfitted with Gaggenau appliances. "Very nice," she crooned.

"Should I take that to mean you like my kitchen?" There was a note of pride in Preston's voice, as if he were talking about one of his children who'd aced an exam.

She met his questioning gaze with a wide smile. "Did you think I was talking about you?"

"I was hoping you'd think I'm nice."

Chandra sobered. "Does it matter what I think of you, Preston?"

"Of course it does. After all, we're going to be collaborating."

"Hold up, dark and brooding. First you want me to develop a paranormal character, and now you're talking about collaboration."

"Pascual is yours, beautiful, and that means we'll have to collaborate to make him a powerful *and* memorable character. I need for him to mesmerize the audience the second he walks on stage. Even before he opens his mouth, he must pull them in and not let them go until the final curtain."

"Are you going to include him in every scene?" Chandra asked.

"No. It would make it too intense. Whenever he's offstage I want to build enough tension for the audience to look forward to his reappearance. Enough shoptalk. I don't know about you, but I'm ready to eat."

Chandra was also ready to eat. Aside from the salad she'd eaten the day before, her only intake of food was a cup of coffee earlier that morning. "It looks as if you do some serious cooking in here."

"It works whenever I host a dinner party. There's more than enough room for a caterer and his staff to work without them bumping into one another."

Preston's kitchen was almost as large as the apartment she was renting from her cousin. It was furnished with top-of-the-line cookware and miscellaneous culinary gadgets suspended on hooks from an overhead rack.

"How often do you have dinner parties?" she asked, recalling Denise telling her that Preston usually kept a low profile.

"I always host one before the debut of a new play. I invite the entire cast and production staff."

She watched as Preston rolled back his shirt cuffs, exposing muscular forearms before washing his hands in one of the double sinks. "How long does it usually take for you to write a play?"

He dried his hands on a towel. "It depends on the subject matter *and* my state of mind. My first one took several years because I'd reworked it half a dozen times. However, there was one I completed in four weeks, but it took its toll on my health because I'd averaged about three hours of sleep each night. I took a couple of months off, checked into a resort and did nothing more strenuous than eat and laze around."

Removing her suit jacket, Chandra hung it on a high-back stool pushed over to the slate-gray granite countertop. "You probably were burned out."

"Probably? I was. It was another year before I was able to focus and write again."

"How long do you project it will take for you to complete *Death's Kiss?*" she asked.

Preston, resting his elbows on the countertop, gave her a long, penetrating stare. "That all depends on my collaborator's availability."

"And that depends on whether I can find a teaching position. I've applied to several schools with vacancies for Pre-K to 6. I'll be available to you until I'm hired."

The schools Chandra had applied to were in designated hard-to-staff districts. Belinda taught at a high school in those districts. Earlier that year one of Belinda's students was arrested and expelled for discharging a handgun in her classroom. Fortunately the incident ended with no casualties.

Teaching in the public school system would be vastly different from what she'd experienced in the exclusive private school in Northern Virginia where the yearly tuition was comparable to private colleges. The most profound difference between the children who attended Cambridge Valley Prep, Philadelphia public schools and her former students in Belize was that the prep school students were the children of elected officials and foreign dignitaries.

Preston stood up straighter. "Where did you teach before?"

"The Peace Corps, and before that I taught at a private school in Virginia."

"You really were in the Peace Corps?" There was a note of incredulity in his query.

"Yes," Chandra confirmed.

"Where were you stationed?" he asked, continuing with his questioning.

"Belize."

Preston never imagined that she had been a Peace Corps volunteer. There was something about Chandra Eaton that projected an air of being cosseted. Now that she'd revealed that she spent two years working in Central America he saw her in a whole new light.

"After you let me know what you want to eat, I want you to tell me about Belize, and if it is as beautiful as the photographs in travel brochures?"

Propping her elbow on the cool surface of the countertop, Chandra supported her chin on her heel of her hand. "I'd like an omelet."

"Would you like a Western, Spanish or spinach?"

"Spinach."

"Blue or goat cheese?"

"I prefer blue cheese." Pushing back from the countertop, Chandra slipped off the stool. "Do you mind if I help you?"

Preston held up a hand. "No. Sit down and relax."

She affected a frown. "I'm not used to sitting and doing nothing."

Preston stared at the slender woman in business attire, realizing they were more alike than dissimilar. Even when he was in between writing projects he always found something to do. He usually retreated to his

Brandywine Valley home to catch up on his reading and watching movies from his extensive DVD collection. He also chopped enough wood to feed two gluttonous fireplaces throughout the winter months. And whenever he heard the stress in his sister's voice from having to deal with her four sons—both sets of twins—he drove down to South Carolina to give her and his probation officer brother-in-law a mini vacation. He took his rambunctious nephews on camping excursions and deep-sea fishing. Last year they'd begun touring the many Sea Islands off the coast of Georgia, Florida and their home state.

Preston enjoyed spending time with the seven- and ten-year-olds, becoming the indulgent uncle, yet oddly had never felt the pull of fatherhood. He wasn't certain if it was because of his own father or because he hadn't met that special woman who would make him reexamine his life and bachelorhood status.

Chandra had thought him a misogynist when he was anything but. He liked women. He liked everything about a woman: her soft skin, the curves of her body and her smell. It was the smell of her skin and hair that was usually imprinted on his brain. Whenever he dated a woman, he was able to pick her out in a darkened room because of her scent.

He preferred working in the kitchen without assistance or interference but decided to relent and let Chandra help him. "Let me get you something to cover your clothes. If you want, you can cut up the fruit."

Chandra flashed a dimpled smile. She needed to do more than sit and watch Preston. She wanted to discover what it was like to actually cook in a gourmet kitchen. "Where's your bathroom?"

Preston pointed to a door at the opposite end of the

kitchen. "It's the door on the right," he said as Chandra headed toward the bathroom.

He stared at the roundness of her shapely hips until she disappeared from his line of vision. *I like her.* Preston liked everything there was to like about Chandra Eaton: her blatant femininity, natural beauty and the intelligence she made no attempt to hide.

When she'd mentioned the idea of writing a play using a vampire as the central character, it had started a flurry of ideas like a trickle of water that flowed into a stream, then into rapids and finally into a fast-flowing river. It reminded him of the Colorado River rushing through the Grand Canyon.

With his creative imagination going full throttle, he was able to outline the production, design the lighting, costumes and props. He could hear the slow drawling Southern cadence and Creole inflections that were as much a part of New Orleans as its cuisine. *Death's Kiss* had come alive in his mind. All that remained was writing it once Chandra developed Pascual.

Preston had taken a package of frozen spinach, four eggs and a plastic container of blue cheese from the refrigerator/freezer as Chandra returned to the kitchen. She was barefoot and had twisted her hair in a loose chignon at the nape of her neck. He smiled when he saw the bright red color on her toes.

Reaching into a drawer under the countertop, he pulled out a bibbed apron. "Come here," he ordered.

Chandra approached Preston, turning so he could slip the apron over her head. He adjusted the length until it reached her knees, then looped the ties twice around her waist.

Shifting, she smiled up at him. "I'm ready, chef."

Lowering his head, Preston kissed the end of her

nose. "Never have I had a more delicious-looking sous chef. If you look in the right side of the refrigerator, you'll find fruit in the lower drawer."

He left Chandra to take care of the fruit salad while he began the task of thawing the spinach in the microwave, placing it in a colander to drain before removing the remaining moisture by squeezing the chopped leaves in cheesecloth. Pausing, he opened an overhead closet and pushed a button on a stereo unit. The beautifully haunting sound of a trumpet filled the duplex.

Chandra shared a smile with Preston as she glanced up from peeling the fuzzy skin of a kiwi, revealing its vibrant green flesh. She found it ironic they had a similar taste in music. Before leaving for Belize, she'd loaded her iPod with music from every genre. Chris Botti's *Night Sessions* had become a favorite.

"You have to have at least one romantic bone in your body if you like Chris Botti," she said teasingly.

Preston stopped mincing garlic on the chopping board. "Okay. I'll admit to having one," he said, conceding.

He didn't know what Chandra meant by being romantic. If it was about sending flowers, telling a woman she looked nice or buying her a gift for her birthday or Christmas, then he would have to say he was. But if a woman expected him to declare his undying love for her then she was out of luck.

He'd asked Elaine to marry him because they'd dated exclusively for three years. It just seemed like the right thing to do. But Elaine wanted more than the flowers, gifts and sex. She wanted his undivided attention whenever she didn't have an acting role. It hadn't mattered if he was working on a new play or directing one slated to go into production. She wanted what she wanted whenever she wanted it.

Preston opened the refrigerator, took out a carafe of freshly squeezed orange juice and a bottle of chilled champagne from a wine storage unit and then returned to the cooking island. There was a soft popping sound when he removed the cork from the bubbly wine. Reaching for two flutes on a rack, he half filled the glasses with orange juice, topping it off with champagne before gently stirring the mixture.

Chandra arranged the fruit in glass dessert bowls. She started with melon balls, adding sliced kiwi, and topped them off with orange sections. The contrasting colors were soft, the fresh fruit inviting.

"Do you want me to set the table?" she asked Preston.

"That can wait until after we toast each other." He handed her a flute, touching his glass to hers. "Here's to a successful collaboration." Their gazes met as they sipped the orange-infused champagne cocktail. She smiled over the rim of the flute.

Chandra let the sweet, tart liquid slide slowly down the back of her throat. "It's delicious."

Preston nodded.

Chandra set down her glass. She didn't want to drink too much before she had a chance to eat. "Where are your dishes?"

"They're in the cabinet over the sink."

"What about coffee or tea?"

"I'll have whatever you have," he said.

"What about juice, chef?"

"I'm not a chef, Chandra."

Preston turned and glared at Chandra, but he couldn't stay angry with her when he saw the humor in her eyes. He was going to enjoy working with her. There was no doubt she was a free spirit if she'd left the States to teach in Belize.

His gaze softened when Chandra swayed to the Latin-infused baseline beats of "All Would Envy" written by Sting and sung by Shawn Colvin.

He took three long strides and pulled her into a close embrace. She fit perfectly within the arc of his arms. They danced as if they'd performed the action countless times. Preston closed his eyes, listening to the words about a wealthy older man who was the envy of other men, old *and* young, because he'd convinced a beautiful young woman to marry him.

Everything about the woman in his arms seeped into him. She was becoming the heroine in *Death's Kiss*. Chandra was right. The play had to have a happy ending. He knew very little about vampires, but he remembered stories about mortals who were bitten by vampires and needed to feed on human blood in order to stay alive.

"Pascual has to be an incredible dancer," Chandra said softly.

"In other words, he must waltz."

Leaning back, she smiled up at Preston. "Yes, but his dance of choice is the tango."

"Where did he learn to tango?" Preston asked.

"In Argentina, of course."

Inky-black eyebrows lifted a fraction. "So, your vampire is from South America?"

"Yes. He's lived there for two centuries, hence his name. He's the son of a noble Spanish landowner and an African slave. Although the tango did not become popular outside of the Argentine ghettos until the early years of the twentieth century, Pascual time travels from one century to another, establishing his reputation as a professional dancer."

Preston angled his head. "I like that you made him mixed race."

"Why's that," Chandra asked.

"Because Josette is also mixed race, and, like her mother, is a free woman of color. I've decided to make her a quadroon, because the character will be easier to cast when I begin auditions. Josette's mother will present her at one of the balls the year she turns sixteen."

"Isn't she rather young?"

Preston twirled Chandra around and around in an intricate dance step. "Not at all. Josette's mother, who is also *plaçée,* made certain her daughter was educated in France, so once she completes her education Josette will be ready to marry and set up her own household."

"Will she meet Pascual at the ball?"

He pondered her question. "No. That would be too contrived. She'll see him for the first time two weeks before the ball when she goes to her dressmaker for a final fitting of her gown. He's there with another woman, who is also a vampire, whom Josette believes is his mistress. Then, she sees him again when she goes to the market with her maid to pick up flowers to decorate the house because her father is coming to share dinner with her mother."

"What happens next, Preston?"

Dipping her low, Preston kissed the end of her nose and then straightened. "No more questions. You will see the play once I begin rehearsals."

Chandra pouted the way she'd done as a child when she hadn't gotten her way. "That's not fair."

He stared at her lush lips. What wasn't fair was that he wanted so much to make love to her, but didn't, because he didn't want to send the wrong message. He'd asked Chandra to work, not sleep with him.

"What's not fair is that you're asking me questions I can't answer because you haven't given me enough information to breathe life into Pascual. You've told me he's an Argentinian of mixed blood and an expert dancer."

Tilting her chin and closing her eyes, Chandra thought of the fantasy man from her erotic dreams. He could've easily become Pascual, coming to her in the dark of the night to make the most exquisite love she'd ever experienced or imagined.

"What are you thinking about?" Preston asked in her ear.

Her eyes opened. "I was trying to imagine Pascual making love to Josette for the first time."

"Before or after she becomes *placée?*"

A beat passed. "Would it add to the conflict if she offers him her virginity?" Chandra asked.

Preston gave Chandra a conspiratorial wink. "It would. But how is she going to convince her white Creole gentleman that she's a virgin?"

"She will confide in her maid, who in turn will ask a voodoo priestess for help. Perhaps you can show a scene with Josette meeting with the voodoo woman. She has great disdain for the woman, but is forced to give up the priceless necklace she's wearing in exchange for a potion that will cause one to fall asleep, and upon waking not remember anything."

He was impressed. Chandra had come up with a credible rationalization for Josette to protect her reputation. After all, the play was to be set in New Orleans.

"Do you want Josette to continue to sleep with Pascual after she becomes *placée,* Chandra?" Preston asked.

Chandra scrunched up her nose. "I see where you're going with this. I think I want Pascual to become her only lover."

"What about her benefactor? Do you think the man will continue to consort with his *plaçée?* There's no way he would be respected in his social circle if word got out that he'd been cuckolded by a woman of color."

"A couple of drops of the potion in a glass of wine each time he comes to visit Josette will eventually take its toll on the poor man when he becomes an amnesiac."

Preston stared at Chandra, and then burst out laughing. He didn't give her a chance to react when he swept her up off the floor, fastening his mouth to hers in an explosive kiss that robbed her of her breath. Her arms went around his neck, she melting against his length when he deepened the kiss.

Chandra's lips parted as she struggled to breathe, giving Preston the slight advantage he needed when the tip of his tongue grazed her palate, the inside of her cheek and curled around her tongue as he made slow, exquisite love to her mouth. The dreams that had plagued her within days of arriving in Belize came to life; she was unable to differentiate between her fantasy lover and Preston Tucker. The familiar flutters that began in her belly moved lower. If he didn't stop, then she knew she would beg him to make love to her.

"Please! No more, Preston."

Preston heard the strident cry that penetrated the sensual fog pulling him under with the force of a riptide. His head popped up, he staring down at Chandra as if seeing her for the first time. The sweep hand on a wall clock made a full revolution before he lowered her until her feet touched the floor.

"I'm sorry, baby."

The skin around Chandra's eyes crinkled when she smiled. "I'm not."

Preston froze. "You're not?"

Going on tiptoe, she kissed his cheek. "You have a very sexy mouth, P.J., and I'd wondered if you knew what to do with it."

A shiver of annoyance snaked its way up his body. Chandra was the first woman who'd let it be known that she was testing his sexual skills.

"Did I pass?"

"Just barely."

Preston's mouth opened and closed several times, and nothing came out. "What did you say?" he asked after he'd collected his wits.

"I said you barely passed." Chandra turned so he wouldn't see her grin. She tried but was unsuccessful when her shoulders shook with laughter. "No!" she screamed when Preston lifted her again, this time holding her above his head as if she were a small child.

"Apologize, Chandra."

"I'm sorry, I'm sorry," she chanted until he lowered her bare feet to the cool tiles.

Still smarting from her teasing, Preston's expression was a mask of stone. "One of these days I'm going to show you exactly what my mouth can do."

"Is that a threat, Preston?"

A smile found its way through his stern-faced demeanor. "No, baby. It was a warning that if you tease me again, then I'm going to expect you to bring it."

His arms fell away and Chandra took a backward step. She didn't know what had gotten into her. She'd known girls who had teased boys they liked, but she hadn't been one of them.

Why now?

And why Preston Tucker?

The questions nagged at her until she dropped her gaze. It'd taken only two encounters with the temperamental playwright to know that he didn't like to be teased or challenged. That meant she had to tread softly and very carefully around him.

"Warning acknowledged."

Chapter 5

Chandra sat across the table from Preston in the kitchen's dining area, enjoying an expertly prepared spinach and blue cheese omelet. Sautéed garlic, olive oil and butter enhanced the subtle flavor of the mild blue cheese, eggs and spinach. Preston had warmed a loaf of French bread to accompany the omelet.

She took a bite of the bread topped off with sweet basil butter. "You missed your calling, P.J.," she said after swallowing. "You should've been a chef."

Preston smiled, staring at Chandra under half-lowered heavy lids. His former annoyance with her teasing him was gone. There was something about her that wouldn't permit him to remain angry. Perhaps it was her lighthearted personality that appealed to his darker, more subdued persona. He was serious, as were his plays which seemed to appeal to the critics. But for the first time since he'd begun writing he was considering one that was fantasy-driven *and* a musical. Since when, he'd asked himself, had he thought of himself as an Andrew Lloyd Webber?

"I'd seriously thought about becoming a chef," he admitted.

"Before you decided to become a playwright?" Chandra asked.

"No. I always wanted to write. I'd like it to be a second or backup career when I decide to give up playwriting."

"Do you think you'll ever stop writing?"

Preston traced the design on the handle of the knife at his place setting with a forefinger. Chandra had asked what he'd been asking himself for years. He loved the process of coming up with a plot and character development. It was sitting through casting calls, ongoing meetings with directors and producers and daily rehearsals before opening night that usually set his teeth on edge. He'd written, directed and produced his last play, thereby alleviating the angst that accompanied a new production.

"That's a question I can't answer, Chandra. I suppose there will become a time when the creative well will dry up."

"Let's hope it's not for a very long time."

"That all depends on my collaborator."

He'd told himself that he would take the next year off and not write—but that was before he found Chandra Eaton's journal in the taxi, and definitely before he met her.

Chandra studied the man sitting opposite her, recognizing an open invitation in his enigmatic dark eyes. "Are you referring to me?"

Preston leaned over the table. "Who else do you think I'm talking about?"

"Did you go to culinary school?" she asked, deftly shifting gears to steer the topic of conversation away from *them* as a couple.

What she and Preston shared was too new to predict beyond their current collaborative project. She'd returned to the States to teach, reestablish her independence and reconnect with her family, not become involved with a man, and especially if that man was celebrity playwright Preston Tucker.

"Why didn't you answer my question, Chandra?"

"I've chosen *not* to answer it because I don't have an answer," she countered with a slight edge to her tone. "Did you go to culinary school?" she asked again.

Preston fumed inwardly. *The stubborn little minx,* he mused. She'd chosen not to answer his query not because she didn't have an answer, but because she hadn't wanted to answer it. He'd never collaborated with another person only because he hadn't had to. *Death's Kiss* was her idea, derived from her suggestion to use a vampire as a central character *and* from her erotic dreams. There was no doubt the play would cause a stir, not only because of the pervasive popularity of vampires in popular fiction, but also because it would be the first time his play would include a musical score.

He would write the play, produce and direct it, which would give him complete control. And if Hollywood wanted to option the work for the big screen then he would make certain his next literary agent would negotiate the terms on his behalf and adhere to his need for creative control.

"I didn't attend culinary school in the traditional sense," he said, answering Chandra's query. "However,

I've taken lots of cooking courses. I spent a summer in Italy learning to prepare some of their regional dishes."

Chandra touched a linen napkin to the corners of her mouth. "Do you speak Italian?"

Preston shook his head. "The classes were conducted in English. How about you? Do you speak another language?"

"I'm fluent in Spanish."

"Did you learn it in Belize?"

"No. I took it in high school and college, and then signed up for a crash course before going abroad. English remains Belize's official language, but Kriol, a Belizean Creole, is the language that all Belizeans speak."

Preston took a sip of herbal tea, enjoying its natural subtle, sweet flavor. He'd enjoyed cooking for Chandra as much as he enjoyed her company. She appeared totally unaffected by his so-called celebrity status. What he'd come to detest were insecure, needy women who wanted him to entertain them, and the woman sitting across from him appeared to be just the opposite.

"What does Kriol sound like?"

"It's a language that borrows words from English, several African languages, a smattering of Spanish and Maya and the Moskito Indian indigenous to the region. *Good morning* in Spanish is *buenas dias*. Creole would be *gud mawnin*. And African-based Garifuna is *buiti binafi*. If you visit the country you'll also hear German and Mandarin."

"It sounds like a real melting pot."

"It is." While staring at Preston, Chandra went completely still. The distinctive voice of Josh Groban filled the kitchen. "He sings beautifully in Spanish."

Preston realized Chandra was listening to the song's lyrics. "What is he saying?"

"*Si volvieras a mi,* means *if you returned to me.*"

"Why do songs always sound so much better when sung in a foreign language?" Preston asked.

"Most songs sound better when you don't understand the words. The love theme from the *Crouching Tiger, Hidden Dragon* sound track is more romantic sung in Chinese than English."

"What are you trying to say?"

Chandra's mind was churning with ideas. "Have your lyricist write at least one song for the play that will be sung in English and Spanish with only a guitar as an accompaniment."

"Should it be a love song?"

She smiled. "But of course.

Preston realized he'd hit the jackpot when he found the journal containing Chandra's erotic dreams. *Death's Kiss* would be a departure from his plays about dysfunctional families and societal woes. He'd won a Tony for the depiction of a psychotic killer who morphs into a sympathetic, repentant character but is denied a stay of execution before the curtain comes down for the final act. Theater critics praised the acting and minimal set decoration, but took the playwright to task for his insinuation of political propaganda in the drama.

His gaze lingered on Chandra, roving lazily over her soft, shining hair to the sweetest lips he'd ever tasted. Her conservative attire artfully disguised a curvy body and a passion he longed to ignite. And there was no doubt Chandra Eaton was a passionate woman as gleaned from the accounts of her dreams. She'd numbered and dated each one, leaving him to ponder how many others she'd had and he hadn't read.

He'd admitted to her that he wasn't a romantic only because he wasn't certain how she'd interpret the word. However, he'd read more than six months of dreams that he could draw upon to make Chandra's vampire a passionate lover.

"How difficult is it to write a play?"

Chandra's query pulled Preston from his reverie. "I thought we were talking about Belize."

She waved a hand. "We can talk about Belize some other time. I want to know about scriptwriting."

"Why? Do you plan on writing one?" he teased with a wide grin.

"Maybe one of these days I'll try my hand at either writing a novel or a play—whichever is easier."

Leaning back in his chair, Preston angled his head. "Anyone can be taught the mechanics of writing, but no one can give an aspiring writer an imagination." He tapped his head with his forefinger. "You have to conjure up plots and characters in your head before you're able to bring them to life on paper."

Chandra thought she detected a hint of censure in Preston's words. Had he believed she wanted to compete with him? "I am not your competition, Preston." She'd spoken her thoughts aloud.

A shadow of annoyance hardened his features. "Do you actually believe I'd think of you as a competitor?"

"If not, then why all the secrecy about not telling me how to write a script?"

"There's no secrecy. And as to competition, the only person I compete with is Preston Japheth Tucker, so don't get ahead of yourself, Miss Eaton."

Chandra sucked her teeth. "Don't start with the bully attitude, P. J. Tucker, because I don't scare easily. Now, are you going to tell me or not?"

Preston stared, unable to form the words to come back at Chandra. She was the complete opposite of any woman he'd ever interacted with. She was as strong and confident as she was beautiful.

"Well, if you put it that way, then I suppose I'd *better* tell you. There's no way I'd be able to explain to my mother that I'd allowed a little slip of a woman to jack me up."

A wave of heat stole its way across Chandra's cheeks. "I wouldn't hit you. In fact, I've never hit anyone in my life." The seconds ticked, and her heart beat a rapid tattoo against her ribs as Preston glared at her.

A slow smile parted Preston's lips, he pointing at her. "Gotcha!"

Pushing back her chair, Chandra came around the table, launching herself at him. He caught her in a split-second motion too quick for the eye to follow. She was sprawled over his knees when his head came down. Covering her mouth with his, Preston robbed her of her breath. The passionate, explosive kiss ended quickly, as quickly as it'd begun.

"Either you have a problem with your short-term memory or you want me to take you upstairs and show you just how romantic I can be. I'm not making an idle threat when I tell you that when I'm finished with you it won't be today, tomorrow or even the next day. I will…" His words trailed off when the telephone rang.

"Excuse me," Preston said as if nothing had passed between him and the woman in his arms.

He stood up, bringing Chandra with him. Instead of releasing her, he held on to her upper arm as he walked over to the wall phone; he tightened his grip when she attempted to extricate herself. Chandra wasn't going anywhere until he settled something with her.

He picked up the receiver. "Hello."

"What's up with you, P.J.?"

Preston took a deep breath, holding it until he felt a band of constriction across his chest. It had taken his agent four days to contact him. "That's what I should be asking you, Cliff. Why the hell did you send me three thousand miles across the country when you knew I wouldn't agree to what the studio heads were proposing? Stop wiggling," he hissed at Chandra.

"Who are you talking to?" Clifford Jessup asked.

"None of your damn business. Now, answer my question, Clifford."

There came a pause. "I thought you would change your mind when you heard what they were offering."

"I thought I told you that the deal wasn't about money, but creative control," Preston said through clenched teeth. "I don't have the time or the inclination to fly to the West Coast for BS. I pay you twenty-five instead of the prevailing fifteen and twenty percent as my literary agent to protect my interests. But apparently you haven't this time. And if I were completely honest, then I'd have to say you haven't looked after my interests in some time."

"What the hell are you trying to say, P.J.?"

"I'm firing you as my literary agent, effective immediately. You'll receive a letter in a few days confirming this. Good luck, Clifford." He replaced the receiver in its cradle with a resounding slam. "What?" he asked Chandra when she stared him. Her mouth had formed a perfect O, and her breasts rose and fell heavily under the silk blouse.

"Are you always so diplomatic?"

"Don't comment on something you know nothing about."

"You're pissed off with me, so you take it out on someone else."

Preston exhaled a breath. "I'm not pissed off with you, Chandra."

Her gaze shifted from his face to his hand clamped around her arm. "No? Then why the caveman grip on my arm, Preston?" He loosened his hold, but not enough for her to escape him.

"I don't want to know anything about the men you're used to dealing with," Preston said in a soft voice that belied his annoyance, "but at thirty-eight I'm a little too old to play games. Especially head games." He leaned in closer. "I like you, Chandra. And it's not about you collaborating with me. You're pretty and you're smart—a trait I admire in a woman, and you're sexy. Probably a lot more sexy than you give yourself credit for. I want to work with you *and* date you."

Chandra couldn't stop the smile stealing its way over her delicate features. "You don't mince words, do you, P.J.?"

"Nope. Too old for that, too, C.E."

Chandra didn't know how to deal with the talented man whose moods ran hot and cold within nanoseconds. "Why should I date you, Preston?"

"Why?" he asked, seemingly shocked by her question. "Didn't I tell you that I'm a nice guy?"

"So you say," she drawled, deciding not to make it easy for him. She wanted to go out with Preston Tucker. In fact, she'd be a fool to reject him. It'd been a long time, entirely too long since she'd found a man with whom she could have an intelligent conversation without watching every word that came out of her mouth. Chandra knew she'd shocked Preston with her off-the-cuff remarks, but she had to know how far she could push him before he pushed back.

It hadn't been that way with Laurence Breslin. They'd dated for a year before he asked her to marry him. However, when she met his parents for the first time they were forthcoming when they expressed their disapproval. They'd always hoped that Laurence would eventually marry the daughter of a couple within their exclusive social circle. To add insult to injury, they'd demanded she return the heirloom engagement ring that had belonged to Laurence's maternal grandmother. Laurence compounded the insult when he forcibly removed the ring from her finger.

"Okay, Preston," she said, smiling, "I'll go out with you."

His eyebrows lifted a fraction. "Why does it sound as if you're doing me a favor?"

"Don't let your ego get the best of you, P.J."

"What are you talking about?"

"You're probably not used to women turning you down."

"Whatever," he drawled.

"Yes or no, Preston?"

"I'm not going to answer that."

Standing on tiptoe, Chandra touched her lips to Preston's. "You don't have to," she whispered, "but there's one question I do expect you to answer for me."

"What's that?" Preston asked, as his lips seared a sensual path along the column of her neck.

Baring her throat, she closed her eyes, reveling in the warmth of his mouth on her skin. "Can I trust you?"

Preston froze as if someone had unexpectedly doused him with cold water. His arms fell to his sides as he glared at Chandra. "You think I'm going to be with you *and* another woman at the same time?"

"I'm not talking about infidelity."

"What are you talking about?"

She stared at a spot over his broad shoulder before her gaze returned to meet his questioning one. "It's about you not lying to me."

"I'd never—"

"Don't say what you won't do," she interrupted. "Just don't do it, Preston."

A beat passed. Preston knew without asking that something had occurred between Chandra and her former fiancé that caused her not to trust him and probably all men. He hadn't slept with so many women that he couldn't remember their names, but whenever they parted it was never because they didn't trust him, and it wouldn't be any different with Chandra.

A sensual smile tilted the corners of his mouth upward. "Now that we've gotten that out of the way, I'd like to take you out to Le Bec-Fin tomorrow night."

Chandra lashes fluttered as she tried to bring her fragile emotions under control. *Maybe he likes you.* Denise's words came back with vivid clarity. Maybe Preston did like her, and not because she was collaborating with him. And despite his literary brilliance and celebrity status she wasn't ready to completely trust him.

Dating Preston Tucker openly would no doubt thrust her into the spotlight for newshounds and the paparazzi, and she had to prepare herself for that. Denise had also revealed that Preston tended to keep a low profile, yet he wanted to take her to a restaurant long considered the best in fine dining. Being seen with him at a fancy, four-star Philadelphia restaurant was hardly what she would consider maintaining a low profile.

"Would you mind if we go another time?"

"Of course I don't mind," he said. "We'll go whenever it's convenient for you."

Chandra decided to flip the script. "How would you like to go out with me tomorrow?"

Preston's eyes narrowed. "I thought you weren't available?"

"I can't have dinner with you because I have a prior engagement. I'm going to Paoli to join my family in celebrating my twin nieces, Sabrina's and Layla's thirteenth birthday."

"You want me to go to a teenage birthday party?"

"No, Preston. You just fired your literary agent, which means you're going to have to replace him. I just thought if you talk to my brother-in-law, perhaps he'll consider representing you."

The impact of his firing his friend and agent weighed heavily on Preston. He hadn't wanted to do it, but Cliff had left him no alternative. If his friend was having personal problems, then he should've confided in him. After all, there were few or no secrets Preston kept from his agent.

But, on the other hand, business was business, and he'd entrusted Clifford to handle his career without questioning his every word or move. Unfortunately, the man had screwed up—big-time and with dire consequences.

"Who is your brother-in-law?"

Chandra flashed a sexy moue, bringing Preston's gaze to linger on her lips. "You'll see tomorrow."

His eyebrows shot up. "You expect me to go with you on a whim?"

"Is that how you see me, Preston?" she spat out. "Now I'm a whim?"

"No, no, no! I didn't mean for it to come out like that."

Crossing her arms under her breasts, Chandra pretended to pout. "Well, it did."

"I'm sorry, Chandra."

She bit back a smile. "Say it like you mean it, Preston."

Preston took a step and pulled her into the circle of his embrace. "I'm sorry, baby." His mellifluous voice had dropped an octave.

Why, Chandra asked herself, hadn't she noticed the rich, honeyed quality of his voice before? It was the timbre of someone trained for the stage.

"Apology accepted. I don't want to tell you my brother-in-law's name because I want you to trust me."

"So, we're back to the trust thing?"

She smiled. "It will always be the trust thing, Preston."

"I thought most women concerned themselves about the love *thang*," he said, teasingly.

"Not with you, P.J. Why would I take up with a man who professes not to be romantic? Women don't need sex from a man as much as they want romance and courtship."

"Maybe I'm going to need a few lessons in that department."

"You're kidding, aren't you?" Chandra asked. "You're thirty-eight years old and you don't know how to romance a woman?"

"What I'm not is romantic," he retorted.

Lowering her arms, she rested her hands on his chest. *"Porbrecito."*

"Which means?"

"You poor thing," she translated.

Preston winked at her. "Now, don't you feel sorry for me?"

"Only a little. However, I'm willing to bet if you follow Pascual's lead you'll do quite well with the ladies."

He wanted to tell Chandra that he was only interested in one lady: her. Not only had she intrigued him but also bewitched him in a way no other woman had. "What time do we leave for Paoli tomorrow?"

"Everyone's expected to arrive around three."

"What time do you want me to pick you up?"

"I'll pick you up at two," Chandra said. Her father would drive her mother in his car, and she would take her mother's car.

"Okay. I want you to relax while I clean up the kitchen. Then we'll go to the office and talk about the play."

"Wouldn't it go faster if I help you?"

Preston glared at Chandra. He'd learned quickly that she wanted to control situations. Well, she was in for a rude awakening. When it came to control of his work he'd unquestionably become an expert.

"Sit down and relax."

She held up her hands. "Okay. You didn't have to go mad hard," she whispered under her breath.

"What did you say?"

"Nothing," Chandra mumbled.

She walked around Preston and sat down at the table. She knew working with him wasn't going to be easy, especially if, without warning, his moods vacillated from hot to cold. What she didn't intend to become was a punching bag for his domineering and controlling personality.

Chandra Eaton was not the same woman who'd left her home and everything familiar and comfortable to work with young children in a region where running water was a priceless commodity.

She'd promised Preston she would help him with his latest play, and she would follow through on her promise—that is until he pushed her to a point where she would be forced to walk away and not look back. It'd happened with a man she'd loved without question, and it could happen again with a man she had no intention of loving.

Chapter 6

Chandra sat between Preston's outstretched legs on a soft leather chaise in a soft butter-yellow shade, wishing she'd worn something a lot more casual. He'd changed into his work clothes: jeans, T-shirt and sandals.

When he'd led her into the home/office Chandra was taken aback with the soft colors, thinking Preston would've preferred a darker, more masculine appeal. Instead of the ubiquitous black, brown or burgundy, the leather sofa, love seats and chaise were fashioned in tones of pale yellow and orange, reminiscent of rainbow sherbet. The citrus shades blended with an L-shaped workstation in a soft vanilla hue with gleaming cherrywood surfaces.

Two walls of floor-to-ceiling built-in bookcases in the same vanilla bean hue were stacked with novels, plays, pamphlets and biographies. Several shelves were dedicated to the many statuettes and awards honoring

Preston's theatrical achievements. She smiled when she saw two Tony awards.

The third wall, covered with bamboolike fabric, was filled with framed citations, diplomas and academic degrees. The last wall was made of glass, bringing in the natural light and panoramic views of the Philadelphia skyline.

Reclining against Preston's chest seemed the most natural thing to do as he explained the notations he'd put down on a legal pad. Chandra squinted, attempting to read his illegible scrawl.

She pointed. "What is that word?"

Preston pressed a kiss to the hair grazing his chin. "You got jokes, C.E.?"

Tilting her chin, Chandra smiled at him over her shoulder. "I'm serious, Preston. I can't decipher it."

He made a face. "She can't decipher *conflict,*" he said sarcastically.

"Hel-lo, P.J. It looks like *confluent* to me."

"I can assure you it *is conflict.* Writing a play is no different from writing a novel or a script for a film or television. It all begins with an idea or premise, a sequence of events, characters and conflict. As the writer I must touch upon all of these elements not only to entice theatergoers to come to see the stage production, but keep them in their seats until the final curtain."

"What's the difference between writing a script for the screen and one for the stage?" Chandra asked.

"Stage plays are much more limited when it comes to the size of the cast, number of settings and the introduction of characters. Whereas with films there can be many, many characters and locales. I try and keep the page count on my plays around one hundred."

"Have you ever exceeded that number?"

"Yes," Preston replied. "But it should never go beyond one hundred twenty pages. The story should concentrate on a few major characters who reveal themselves through dialogue, unlike a film actor who will utilize dialogue and physical action."

Shifting slightly, Chandra met Preston's eyes. "When do you know if your premise is a play or a film?"

"The key word is physical action. If I imagine a story and I see it as frames of images, then it's a play. But, if the images are filled with physical action, then it's a film script."

"So, you see *Death's Kiss* as a play?"

"It can go either way. As a film it probably would be darker, more haunting, the characters of Pascual and Josette more complex, and there would be more physical action than on the stage."

"What would the rating be if you wrote the screenplay?"

"Probably a PG-13," he said.

His response surprised Chandra. "Why not an R rating?"

"An R rating would be at the studio's discretion. I always believe you can sell more tickets with a PG-13 rating than one that's rated R or NC-17."

"Is that why you insist on literary control?" she asked, continuing with her questioning.

Preston nodded. "That's part of it. What you and I have to decide on is the backstory for *Death's Kiss*."

"Would I need a backstory for a mythical character?"

"Do you want Pascual to feed on blood in order to survive? If not, then what are his family background, education, social and political beliefs? Is he in favor or opposed to slavery?"

A look of distress came over Chandra's face. "I don't want the play to focus on slavery, because it's a too-painful part of our country's history."

"It will *not* focus on slavery, but a peculiar practice germane but not limited to New Orleans and the descendants of *gens de couleur.* I've done some research," Preston continued, "uncovering that it was acceptable behavior for a white man to take a slave as young as twelve as his lover. It would prove beneficial to the woman if she produced children. She would be emancipated along with their offspring. Josette's mother is a free woman of color, thereby making her free."

"Where does Josette's father live?"

"Etienne Fouché has a plantation twenty miles outside of New Orleans where he lives with his white family, and he also has an apartment within the city where he entertains his friends. Then, there's a Creole cottage he'd purchased for his *plaçée* and Josette only blocks from his apartment. He will spend a few months with his legitimate wife, but most of his time will be spent within the city.

"France has declared its independence and the Louisiana territory has been ceded to the United States. The first act will open with Josette returning to the States from France and her mother telling her she must prepare for the upcoming ball. However, the Josette who returns at sixteen isn't the same naive and cosseted girl who'd cried incessantly when she boarded a ship to take her to Paris four years before. She is also educated, while it was illegal to teach blacks to read and write in the States. She doesn't believe in *plaçage,* wants to choose her own husband, and her opposition results in conflict because her mother has promised her to the son of one of the largest landowners in the region. Within minutes of the opening act…"

Preston's words trailed off when he saw that Chandra had closed her eyes, while her chest rose and fell in an even rhythm. "Chandra," he said softly, "did you fall asleep on me?"

"No. I was listening to you. Champagne always makes me drowsy."

"We can stop now if you want to."

Chandra smiled, but didn't open her eyes. "Do you mind if we don't move?"

Shifting slightly, he settled her into a more comfortable position. "We can stay here all night if you want."

She opened her eyes. "No, Preston. I'm not ready to sleep with you."

Preston twirled several strands of her hair around his finger. "I wasn't suggesting we sleep together. The bedrooms on the second floor are for my guests."

"Where do you sleep?" Chandra asked quickly, hoping to cover up her faux pas. Preston had kissed her twice and she'd assumed that he wanted to sleep with her. If she could have, at that moment she would've willed herself totally invisible.

"Here on the chaise. The sofa converts into a bed, but half the time I end up sleeping on it instead of in it."

"I hope you have a chiropractor." Preston's height exceeded the length of the sofa by several inches.

"I happen to have one on speed dial. Sitting for hours in front of a computer takes a toll on the neck, back and shoulders."

"You should practice yoga or tai chi," Chandra suggested. "I find it works wonders whenever I have trouble sleeping."

Preston was hard-pressed not to smile. Chandra had just given him the opening he needed to delve into her dreams without letting her know he'd read and committed to memory what she'd written in the journal he'd found.

"What would keep you from sleeping?" he asked.

"It's usually anxiety or a very overactive imagination."

"What do you have to be anxious about, Chandra?"

She exhaled an audible sigh. "A couple of weeks before I was scheduled to leave for Belize, I discovered I couldn't sleep. I'd go to bed totally exhausted, but couldn't sleep more than one or two hours. My dad, who is a doctor, offered to write a scrip for a sedative, but I refused because I didn't want to rely on a controlled substance that could possibly lead to dependency.

"I was losing weight and when I ran into a friend from college I told her about my problem. She was on her way to a yoga class so I went along just to observe. I joined the class the following day, and also signed up for tai chi."

"How long did it take for you to get rid of your insomnia?"

Chandra stared at the vivid color on her toes. "It took about two weeks. By the time I'd arrived in Belize I was sleeping soundly, but then something else happened."

Lowering his head, Preston pressed his nose to her hair, inhaling the sweet fragrance. "What happened?"

The seconds ticked, bringing with them a comfortable silence. "I began dreaming."

The admission came from a place Chandra hadn't known existed. Her dreams were a secret—a secret she never planned to divulge to anyone. She'd recorded her dreams in journals, believing she would one day reread them. She'd thought about publishing them under a pseudonym, because some of them were more than sensual. They were downright erotic.

"Were they dreams or nightmares?"

"Oh, they were dreams."

Preston smiled. Her dreams had become his nightmares because they'd kept him from a restful night's sleep. "How often did you dream?"

"I had them on average of two to three a week."

"Whenever I dream I usually don't remember what they were," Preston admitted.

"It's different with me," Chandra said. "Not only do I remember, but they were so vivid that I was able to write them down."

"What do you think triggered your dreams?"

"I don't know, Preston."

"Are your dreams different, or all along the same train of thought?"

Chandra didn't know how much more she could divulge about her dreams before Preston realized that she was sexually frustrated, that it had been years since she'd slept with a man. And she didn't need a therapist to tell her that she'd used her dreams to act out her sexual fantasies.

"They were the same," she finally admitted.

"That sounds boring, C.E."

She rolled her eyes. "My dreams were hardly boring, P.J."

"Do you want to tell me about them?" Preston whispered in her ear.

"No!"

Preston fastened his mouth to the side of her neck. "Why not?"

Chandra shivered slightly when Preston increased the pressure along the column of her neck. A slight gasp escaped her parted lips with the growing hardness pressing against her hips. It took Herculean strength not to move back to experience the full impact of Preston's erection.

"What are you doing, Preston?" Chandra questioned, not recognizing the strangled voice as her own.

Closing his eyes while swallowing a groan, Preston tried to think about any and everything except the soft crush of Chandra's buttocks pressed intimately to his groin.

"I'm committing your scent to memory."

Chandra closed her eyes. "I'm not talking about you nibbling on my neck."

"What are you talking about?"

"Pascual would never hump Josette."

"I'm not humping you, baby. This is humping." Preston gyrated back and forth, pushing his erection against her hips.

Waves of desire swept over Chandra like a desert sirocco, stealing the breath from her lungs and stopping her heart for several seconds. The sensations holding her in an erotic grip were similar to what she'd experienced in her dreams. Her breasts were heavy, the area between her thighs moist and throbbing with a need that screamed silently to be assuaged.

The man who came to her in her dreams was a fantasy, a nameless, faceless specter she'd conjured up from the recesses of her overactive imagination, but Preston Tucker was real, as real as his heat *and* arousal.

"Please don't move." Chandra was pleading with him, but she was past caring, because if he didn't stop then she would beg him to make love to her. It was one thing to fantasize about making love with a faceless specter and another to have an actual live, red-blooded man simulating making love to her.

Preston went still, but there was little he could do to still the pulsing sensations in his groin. He didn't know what it was about Chandra Eaton that had him so lacking in self-control. He'd wanted to rationalize and tell himself it was because of her erotic dreams, but he would be lying to himself. He'd told Chandra that he liked her. The truth was he liked her *and* wanted her in his bed; however the notion of sleeping with Chandra was shocking and totally unexpected.

"What were we talking about before you decided to hump me, Preston?"

The soft, dulcet voice broke into his reverie. "We were talking about your dreams."

"Even before that," Chandra said in an attempt to change the topic. Preston had asked what she'd dreamed about, and how could she tell him that her dreams were *all* about sex, that they were continuous frames of R- and X-rated films with her in the leading role.

"We were discussing Josette's father."

"Will he have legitimate children?"

Wrapping an arm around Chandra's waist, Preston shifted her to a more comfortable position. His erection had gone down and her body was more relaxed, pliant. "No. His wife gave him a daughter, but she died from a fever before she turned two. Since then she has had several miscarriages, thereby leaving him without a legitimate heir."

"Is Etienne Fouché wealthy?"

"Very," Preston confirmed. "He'd bought out a

neighboring planter and is now the owner of the largest sugarcane plantation in St. Bernard parish."

"How is Etienne's relationship with his wife?" Chandra asked.

"They're cordial. Theirs is a marriage of convenience. Madame Fouché is what one could call homely, so her father offered Etienne a sizable dowry to marry his daughter. Madame Fouché, who has an aversion to sex, is overjoyed when her doctor tells her that her husband must not share her bed again. She spends most of her free time entertaining the wives of other planters and/ or spending the summers in Europe to escape the heat and fevers that claim thousands of lives each year."

Sitting up straighter, Chandra turned to stare up at Preston. "You've made Etienne a gentleman farmer who derives his wealth from slaves who grow and process white gold."

"The geographic location and family background are key elements of the backstory. I could've easily made him a professional gambler, but how would that work for Josette and her mother. A gambler who could win or lose a fortune with the turn of a single card. And if he found himself without funds, then he would use their home as collateral. I know you don't want to touch on the slavery issue, but remember we're dealing with free people of color.

"As the writer I'm totally absorbed in the lives of the characters until the play is completed. Then it becomes the director's responsibility to get his actors to bring them to life on stage."

Chandra swiveled enough so that she was practically facing Preston. "Do you know who you want to direct *Death's Kiss?*" A smile softened his mouth, bringing her gaze to linger on the outline of his sensual lower lip. "What are you smiling about?"

"I'm going write, direct *and* produce *Death's Kiss.*"

"Total control," she whispered under her breath.

Preston's eyebrows lifted. "Do you have a problem with my decision, C.E.?"

Silence filled the room as Chandra boldly met his eyes. Missing was the warmth that lurked there only moments before. "It's your play, Preston, so you can do whatever you want with it."

"It's not only my play, Chandra."

"Who else does it belong to, if not you, Preston."

"Pascual is your character."

"And *Death's Kiss* is your play," she countered. Chandra pushed to her feet. "I'm going to head home now. Based on what you've told me about Etienne and Josette, I'm going to have to revise my first impression of Pascual."

Preston knew Chandra was smarting about his decision to write, direct and produce the play. What she didn't understand was that he knew his characters better than anyone, and he hadn't wanted to explain their motivation to a tyrannical director who insisted on having his way. He'd lost count of the number of times he'd had to bite his tongue so as not to lose his financial backing.

He moved off the chaise. "Don't stress yourself too much. It will probably be another month before we flesh out the entire cast of characters."

Nodding, Chandra turned and walked out of the office. "I'll see you tomorrow at two."

"I'll be downstairs."

She entered the kitchen, pushing her feet into her

shoes before reaching for her suit jacket. "Dress is casual."

Resting his hands on her shoulders, Preston turned Chandra around to face him. "Thank you for coming. I really enjoyed your company."

Chandra was momentarily shocked into speechlessness. Preston thanking her for her company spoke volumes. Despite his brilliance, fame, awards and financial success, Preston J. Tucker was a private and a lonely man.

A hint of a smile parted her lips when she stared into his fathomless dark eyes. "Thank you for inviting me."

Preston didn't want Chandra to leave, but he didn't want to embarrass himself and communicate that to her. "I'll call the driver and have him bring the car around."

Going on tiptoe, Chandra touched her lips to his. "Thank you."

They shared a smile as she slipped her hand into his. They were still holding hands during the elevator ride to the building lobby and out onto the sidewalk where the driver stood with the rear door open.

She slid onto the rear seat and waved to Preston. He returned her wave before the driver closed the door and rounded the Town Car to take his place behind the wheel.

Chandra turned to stare over her shoulder out the back window to find Preston standing on the sidewalk. His image grew smaller and smaller then disappeared from view when the driver turned the corner.

A knowing smile softened her mouth when she shifted again. *I like him.* "I like him," she repeated under her breath, as if saying it aloud would make it more real.

Chapter 7

Chandra maneuvered her car to the curb of the high-rise, tapping lightly on the horn to garner Preston's attention. He was dressed in a lightweight, navy blue suit, white shirt and black slip-ons. Her eyebrows lifted slightly when she spied the two small colorful shopping bags he held in his left hand.

He rounded the car to the driver's side and dipped his head to peer through the open window. "I'll drive. I do know how to get to Paoli," Preston added when Chandra gave him a quizzical look. Reaching in, he unlocked the door, opened it and helped her out. Three inches of heels put the top of her head at eyelevel. His penetrating gaze took in everything about her in a single glance: lightly made-up face, luxurious dark brown hair secured in a ponytail, black stretch tank top, matching stretch cropped pants and high-heeled mules. He brushed a kiss over her cheek. "You look very cute."

Heat feathered across her face with his unexpected compliment. She'd changed her outfits twice. When she'd gotten up earlier that morning, the mercury was already sixty-eight, and meteorologists were predicting temperatures to peak in the mid-eighties. Chandra much preferred the Indian summer weather to the near-freezing temperatures because she knew it would take her a while to adjust to the climate change.

Her eyes met Preston's as the skin around his penetrating gaze lingered briefly on her face before slipping lower to her breasts. "Thank you."

Preston's lips parted in a smile as he reached over with his free hand and tugged gently on her ponytail. "You're quite welcome." He led her around the Volvo, seated her and then retraced his steps once she'd fastened her seat belt.

He took off his suit jacket, placing it and the shopping bags on the rear seat. Sitting behind the wheel, he adjusted the seat to accommodate his longer legs, noting that Chandra had already programmed her trip into the GPS.

"What's in the shopping bags?" Chandra asked when Preston maneuvered into the flow of traffic.

"It's just a little something for your nieces."

She frowned. "You didn't have to bring anything."

Preston's frown matched hers. "I couldn't show up empty-handed."

"Yes, you could, Preston. You're my guest."

"That may be true, but I feel better bringing something. After all, it's not every day someone turns thirteen. Your nieces are no longer tweens, but bona fide teenagers. And I'm willing to bet they'll be quick to remind everyone of that fact."

Chandra's frown disappeared. "You're right. When I

spoke to my sister earlier this morning, she told me that was the first thing they said."

"Do you remember being thirteen?" Preston asked.

She shook her head. "No. Every year was a blur until I turned eighteen."

"What happened that year?"

"I left home for college."

"Where did you go?"

"Columbia University."

"Was Columbia your first choice?"

Chandra stared through the windshield. "No. I was seriously considering going to the University of Pennsylvania, then decided an out-of-state school was a better choice if I wanted to stretch my wings."

Preston gave Chandra a sidelong glance before returning his gaze to the road. "Mom and Dad didn't want their baby to leave the nest? Yes or no?" he asked when she glared at him.

"No," she said after a prolonged pause. "I decided to go away because my brother and sisters went to in-state colleges. I wanted to be the one to break the tradition."

"Where did—" The chiming of the cell phone attached to his belt preempted what he intended to say. Preston removed the phone, taking a furtive look at the display. "Excuse me, Chandra, but I need to take this call."

She nodded, smiling. "It's okay."

He pressed a button, activating the speaker feature. "Hey, Ray. Thanks for getting back to me."

"What's up, P.J.?" asked a raspy voice.

"How's your schedule?" Preston asked.

A sensual chuckle filled the car. "What do you need, P.J.?"

"I need a score for a new play with an early nineteenth-century New Orleans setting." He shared a smile with Chandra when she winked at him. "It's a dramatic musical."

A pregnant silence filled the interior of the vehicle. "Did you say musical?"

"Yes, I did."

"Hold up, prince of darkness," Ray teased, laughing. "Don't tell me you're going soft."

"It's nothing like that, Ray."

"What happened?"

"I'm collaborating with someone who convinced me to leave the dark side for my next project."

"Good for her."

"How do you know it's a she?" Preston asked.

"I know you too well, P.J. If she was a *he,* and if it's a musical, then it wouldn't have been about nineteenth, but twenty-first-century New Orleans." His *New Orleans* sounded like *Nawlins.*

Preston wanted to tell Ray that he didn't know him *that* well. It had been the same with Clifford Jessup. Cliff had felt so comfortable managing his business affairs that he'd found himself with one less client.

"Can you spare some time where we can get together to talk about what I want?" he asked instead.

"I'm free tomorrow. I'd rather get together at your house. Beth isn't due for another two weeks, but she's been complaining about contractions. I don't want to be too far away if and when she does go into labor."

The reason Preston had moved into the city was not to conduct business out of his home, but with Ray's wife's condition he would make an exception. "That's not a problem. Better yet, bring Beth with you. If the warm weather holds, we can cook and eat outdoors."

The lyricist met his artist wife when they were involved in a summer stock production written by a Bucks County playwright. Ray had written the songs, while Beth designed the set decorations. It was love at first sight, and they married two months later. They'd recently celebrated their tenth wedding anniversary, and now were expecting their first child.

"It would do Beth good to get out of the house," Ray remarked.

"How does one o'clock sound to you?" Preston asked.

"One is good. We'll see you tomorrow."

Preston smiled. "One it is." He ended the call, placing the phone on the console between the seats. Following the images on the GPS, he made a left turn on the road leading to Paoli. "Will you join me tomorrow?"

Preston's query was so unexpected that Chandra replayed it in her head. She stared at his distinctive profile for a full minute. "You want me to join you where?"

"I have a house in Kennett Square, and I'd like you to be present when I meet with Ray Hardy."

She sat up straighter, all of her senses on full alert. "Are you talking about *the* Raymond Hardy?"

"Yes. Since you suggested a musical, then I'll leave the music portion of the play up to you."

Chandra felt her pulse quicken. Raymond Hardy had been compared to British lyricist Sir Tim Rice, whose collaboration with composer Sir Andrew Lloyd Webber had earned them countless awards and honors in the States and across the pond.

She gave Preston a skeptical look. "You're kidding, aren't you?"

"No. My task will be to write the dialogue, while the music will be at your discretion."

"But…but I can't write music or lyrics," she sputtered.

"That will be Ray's responsibility. What I want you to do is tell him what you want. Ray is amazing. Give him an idea of what you want, and within a couple of hours he will have a song written in its entirety."

Chandra chewed her lower lip. She was being thrust into a situation where there was no doubt she would be in over her head. And it had all begun with her leaving her journal in a taxi where Preston Tucker had found it. If she'd retrieved her journal and not remarked about Preston's work, then she wouldn't be faced with the quandary of whether she wanted to become inexorably entwined in the lives of an award-winning dramatist and lyricist.

"You're going to have to let me know a little more about the plot," she said, stalling for time.

"We'll either discuss it tonight or tomorrow morning."

"When are we going to have time tonight, Preston? We probably won't leave my sister's house until at least eight or nine. And, remember it's at least an hour's drive between Philly and Paoli."

Reaching over, Preston rested his right arm over the back of Chandra's seat. "Don't stress yourself, baby. You can spend the night with me, which means we can stay up late."

Chandra looked at him as if he'd taken leave of his senses. "I can't spend the night with you."

A soft chuckle began in Preston's chest before it filled the interior of the Volvo. "Don't tell me you're worried about your virtue, Miss Independent. Didn't I tell you that you're safe with me, Chandra?"

His teasing her made Chandra feel like a hapless ingenue instead of a thirty-year-old woman who'd left home at eighteen to attend college in New York. When she returned it wasn't to put down roots in her home state, but in Virginia. Then she'd left the States to teach in a Central American country for a couple of years. She was currently living with her parents but that, too, was temporary; she was estimating she would move into her cousin's co-op before the end of the month.

She rolled her eyes at Preston. "Nothing's going to happen that I don't want to happen."

"There you go," he drawled. "After we leave Paoli I'll drive back to my place to pick up my car, then I'll follow you back home, so you can get what you need for a couple of days."

"A couple of days, Preston! When did overnight become a couple of days?"

"There's no need to throw a hissy fit, Chandra." His voice was low, calm, much calmer than he actually felt. "I need as much of your input as possible before you go back to work."

He didn't want to tell her that he wanted to begin working on the play before the onset of winter—his least productive season when there were days when his creative juices literally dried up.

"Okay," Chandra agreed after a comfortable silence. She was committed to helping Preston with the play, and she planned to hold up her end of the agreement. "But I'm going to have to use your computer to check my e-mail."

"That's not going to present a problem. I have both

a laptop and desktop at the house. Do you have to ask your parents if you can stay out overnight?"

Chandra rolled her eyes, then stuck out her tongue at Preston. "Very funny," she drawled sarcastically.

He smothered a grin. "You better watch what you do with that tongue."

"What are you talking about?"

"I have the perfect remedy for girls who offer me their tongues."

She rolled her eyes again. "I *ain't* scared of you, P. J. Tucker."

"I don't want you to be, C.E., because I intend for us to have a lot fun working together."

"I hope we can."

Preston gave her a quick sidelong glance. "Why do you sound so skeptical?"

"You're controlling, Preston."

"And you're not?" he countered.

"A little," Chandra admitted.

"Only a little, C.E.? You're in denial, beautiful. You are very, very controlling. If it can't be your way, then it's no way."

Resting a hand on her hip, Chandra shifted, as far as her seat belt would permit her, to face Preston. Her eyes narrowed. "Do you really think you know me that well?"

Preston longed to tell Chandra that he knew more about her than she realized, that he knew she was a passionate woman with a very healthy libido.

"I only know what you've shown me," he stated solemnly. "There's nothing wrong with being independent or in control as long as you let a man be a man."

"In other words, you expect me to grovel because you're the celebrated Preston Tucker."

Preston shook his head. "No."

"Then, what is it you want?"

"I want us to get along, Chandra. We may not agree on everything, but what I expect is compromise. I grew up hearing my parents argue every day, and I vowed that I would never deal with a woman I had to fight with. It's too emotionally draining. I began writing to escape from what I had to go through whenever my father came home.

"He would start with complaining about his boss and coworkers, and then it escalated to his nervous stomach and why he didn't want to eat what my mother had cooked for dinner. Most times she didn't say anything. She'd take his plate and empty it in the garbage before walking out of the kitchen. My sister and I would stare at our plates and finish our dinner. Then we would clear the table, clean up the kitchen and go to our respective bedrooms for the night. I always finished my homework before dinner, so that left time for me to write."

"Did your father have a high-stress job?"

"He was an accountant, who'd had his own practice but couldn't keep any employees."

Chandra couldn't remember her parents arguing, and if they did then it was never in front of their children. Between his office hours, house visits and working at the local municipal hospital, Dwight Eaton coveted the time he spent with his family.

"Did he verbally abuse his employees?"

A beat passed. "Craig Tucker was what psychologists call passive-aggressive. Most people said he was sarcastic. I thought of him as cynical and mocking."

Now Chandra understood why Preston sought to

avoid acerbic verbal exchanges. "Are your parents still together?"

Another beat passed as a muscle twitched in Preston's lean jaw. "No. My dad died twenty-two years ago. He'd just celebrated his fortieth birthday when he passed away from lung cancer. He'd had a two-pack-a-day cigarette habit. My mother may have given in to my father's demands in order to keep the peace, but put her foot down when she wouldn't let him smoke in the house or car. He would sit on a bench behind the house smoking whether it was ninety-five degrees or twenty-five degrees. I found it odd that my mother didn't cry at his funeral, but it was years later that I came to realize Craig Tucker was probably suffering from depression."

Preston's grim expression vanished like pinpoints of sun piercing an overcast sky. "He did in death what he wouldn't do in life. He gave my mother a weekly allowance to buy food, while he paid all the bills. If she ran out of money, then she had to wait for Friday night when he placed an envelope with the money on the kitchen table. He was such a penny-pincher that my sister called him Scrooge behind his back. Well, Scrooge had invested heavily *and* wisely, leaving my mother very well off financially. He'd also set aside monies for me and my sister's college fund. Yolanda went to Brown, while I went to Princeton.

"After I graduated, my mother sold the house and moved back to her hometown of Charleston, South Carolina, enrolled in the College of Charleston and earned a degree in Historic Preservation and Community Planning. Then, she applied to and was accepted into a joint MS degree in Historic Preservation with Clemson. With her education behind her, she opened a small shop selling antiques and reproductions of Gullah artifacts.

Her basket-weaving courses have a six-month waiting list."

Chandra's mouth curved into an unconscious smile. Preston's mother had to wait to become a widow to come into her own. Her adage was always Better Late Than Never.

"I remember my parents driving down to Florida one year, and when we went through South Carolina I saw old women sitting on the side of the road weaving straw baskets. I'm sorry we didn't stop to buy at least one."

"That's too bad," Preston remarked, "because the art of weaving baskets has been threatened with the advance of coastal development. Those living in gated subdivisions wouldn't let the weavers come through to pluck the sweetgrass they coil with pine needles, bulrushes and palmetto fronds used to make the baskets. Thankfully the true center of sweetgrass basket weaving is flourishing in Mount Pleasant, a sea island near the Cooper River."

"It sounds as if your mother has found her niche," Chandra said in a soft voice, filled with a mysterious longing.

"If not her niche, then her passion. Last year she met a man who teaches historical architecture and sits on the Charleston Historic Preservation and Community Planning board. I've never known my mother to laugh so much as when she's with him. She moved in with him at the beginning of the year."

"Good for her."

A wide grin creased Preston's face. "If you're talking about a romance novel, then Rose Tucker is truly a heroine."

"Is she going to marry her hero?"

"I don't know. I think she's still a little skittish about

marriage, because she hasn't sold her condo. They divide their time living at his house during the week, and come into the city to stay at her condo on the weekend. It doesn't bother me or Yolanda if they never marry, as long as they're happy."

"Where does your sister live?" Chandra knew she was asking Preston a lot of questions, but she'd come to appreciate the sound of his sonorous baritone voice.

Settling back against the leather seat, she closed her eyes when he talked about his older sister, his brother-in-law and two sets of identical twin nephews. Again, she wondered why he hadn't married and fathered children when he told of the outings with his nephews. She opened her eyes when he patted her knee.

"Tell me about your family so I know what to expect."

Chandra recognized landmarks that indicated they were only blocks from her sister's house. "Too late. We're almost there."

Preston groaned aloud when the voice coming from the GPS directed him to turn right at the next street. He'd wanted Chandra to brief him as to her relatives. "Did you tell your folks you were bringing a guest?"

"Nope."

Decelerating, he maneuvered into a parking space across the street from a three-story Colonial. "Did they expect you to bring a guest?"

Chandra unbuckled her seat belt. "If you're asking whether I normally attend family functions with a man, then the answer is no. It's been more than three years since I've had a serious boyfriend."

Smiling, Preston rested his right arm over the back of her seat. "So, I'm your boyfriend?"

She flashed an attractive moue. "No, P.J., you're a friend."

He leaned closer. "Do you think I'll ever be your boyfriend?"

Chandra leaned closer until she was inhaling the moist warmth of Preston's breath. "You can if..."

"If what?" he whispered.

"You can if I can trust you."

Preston froze. "What's with you and the trust thing?"

"It's very important to me, Preston. Without trust there can be no boyfriend, girlfriend, no relationship."

He smiled. "Are you amenable to something that goes beyond platonic?"

Chandra blinked. "I am, but only—"

"If you can trust me," he said, completing her sentence.

"Yes."

Preston angled his head, pressing his mouth to Chandra's, reveling in the velvety warmth of her parted lips. It had been years since he'd sat in a car kissing a woman but there was something about Chandra Eaton that made him feel like an adolescent boy. First it was the unexpected erection after reading her erotic dreams and now it was having her close.

"You have my solemn vow that I will never give you cause to mistrust me."

Chandra quivered at the gentle tenderness of the kiss, and in that instant she wanted to trust Preston not because she wanted to but needed to. Every man she'd met after Laurence had become a victim of her acerbic tongue and negative attitude whenever they'd expressed an interest in her.

She'd loved Laurence, expecting to spend the rest

of her life with him, but when he caved under pressure from his family, her faith in the opposite sex was shattered—almost beyond repair. However, Preston Tucker was offering a second chance. She didn't expect marriage, not because he was a confirmed bachelor, but because it didn't figure into her short-term plans.

Chandra wanted to secure a teaching position, settle into her new residence, and dating Preston would become an added bonus. "I believe you," she whispered, succumbing to the forceful, drugging possession of his lips. It was with supreme reluctance that she ended the kiss. "Let's stop before one of the kids see us. I don't want to send my nieces the wrong message, that it's okay to make out in a car."

Preston's lids lowered, he successfully concealing his innermost feelings from the woman he wanted to make love to with a need that bordered on desperation. He knew it was her beauty, poise, intelligence and sensuality that fueled his obsession.

"The curtain just came down on the first act."

Chandra smiled up at him through her lashes. "When do we begin act two?"

"Tonight."

Chapter 8

*T*onight. The single word reverberated in Chandra's head as she led the way toward the rear of the house where her sister lived with her husband and their nieces. The sound of voices raised in laughter greeted her and Preston when they walked into an expansive patio overlooking an inground pool. Her parents were holding court with their granddaughters and grandson, Myles and Zabrina lay together on a webbed lounger by the pool and Griffin stood at the stove in the outdoor kitchen with an arm around Belinda's waist. A long rectangular table with seating for twelve and a smaller table with half that amount were set up under a white tent.

Chandra stopped short, causing Preston to plow into her back; she saw someone she hadn't expected to see. Sitting under an umbrella with Denise was Xavier Eaton. The last time she'd seen her cousin was days before he was to begin his tour of duty in Afghanistan.

"I'll introduce you to everyone after I talk to someone," she whispered to Preston.

Arms outstretched and grinning from ear to ear, she walked into Xavier's embrace when he stood up. She found herself crushed against a rock-hard chest. "Welcome home, Captain Eaton."

"It's now Major Eaton. I'd pick you up, but I have a bum leg."

Pulling back, Chandra saw that he was supporting himself with a cane. She hadn't realized her cousin, dressed in civilian clothes and looking more like a male model than a professional soldier, had sustained an injury. She'd lost count of the number of women who'd asked her to introduce them to Xavier. He was always polite to them, while smoothly rejecting further advances. He had also earned the reputation of remaining friends with his former girlfriends.

What they didn't know was that he had a mistress. Xavier Phillip Eaton ate, breathed and slept military. He'd attended military prep school, graduated and then enrolled at The Citadel, The Military College of South Carolina. He continued his military education when he was accepted into the Marine Corps War College. After 9/11 he was deployed to Iraq. He completed one tour of duty before he was sent to Afghanistan.

"Is it serious?"

"It will heal."

"That's not what I asked, Xavier."

Xavier leaned in closer. "If you're asking if I'm going to be a cripple, then the answer is no."

Narrowing her gaze, Chandra decided to drop the subject. Tiptoeing, she kissed his smooth cheek. "We'll talk later." Shifting slightly, Chandra beckoned Preston closer, reaching for his hand as he approached. "Preston,

I'd like for you to meet my cousin, Xavier Eaton. Xavier, Preston Tucker."

Xavier offered his hand. "Why does your name sound so familiar?"

Denise Eaton stood up, looping her arm around her brother's waist. "That's because he's Preston Tucker, the playwright."

Xavier pumped Preston's hand vigorously. "I'm honored to meet you." He gave him a rough embrace, while slapping him on the back with his free hand.

Chandra caught Denise's look of expectation. "Preston, this is Xavier's sister, Denise."

Denise managed to disentangle herself from her brother, shyly extending her hand. Her large dark eyes shimmered like polished jet, while flyaway black curls took on a life of their own whenever she moved her head. A shaft of sunlight fell across her heart-shaped face, highlighting the yellow-orange undertones in her flawless brown face. She was a softer, prettier, feminine version of Xavier.

"Mr. Tucker. I've seen and read every play you've written."

Preston took her hand, squeezing it gently. "Please, no Mr. Tucker. Call me Preston."

Chandra didn't know how, but she knew Preston was uncomfortable with his celebrity status. She rested a hand on his shoulder. "Now I'll introduce you to my sister and brother-in-law."

Preston fell in step with Chandra, feeling the heat of the eyes that followed him as he walked across the patio. "Is Griffin Rice your brother-in-law?"

Chandra stopped suddenly, staring at Preston as if he were a stranger. She'd wanted it to be a surprise, but apparently he'd turned the tables. "Yes, Griffin *is* my brother-in-law."

Preston dipped his head, brushing a kiss on her mouth. "Good looking out, beautiful." Amid a chorus of coughs and cleared throats his head popped up as a smile softened the angles in his face. "Good afternoon."

Griffin Rice came forward, hand outstretched. Today he wore a white T-shirt, jeans and running shoes. He looked nothing like the man who had graced the cover of *GQ*. As the attorney for some of sports biggest superstars, he had become a superstar in his own right whenever he escorted models and actresses to social and sporting events. His gorgeous face and distinctive cleft chin made him a magnet for women everywhere. When the news got out that he'd married Belinda Eaton the gossip columnists scrambled to uncover everything about the woman who'd snared one of the country's most eligible bachelors.

"P. J. Tucker. You old dog! When did you hook up with my sister-in-law?"

Preston and Chandra shared a smile. "We got together after she got back from Belize." He handed Griffin the colorful shopping bags. "These are for Layla and Sabrina."

"How do you know Preston?" Chandra asked Griffin.

"We worked together on a fundraiser a few years back. Your boyfriend put the squeeze on some of his well-heeled friends to reach our goal to set up an after-school sports program for some kids in North Philly."

Preston and Griffin shook hands. "I had to do everything short of bringing out a rubber hose to make them dig deep for a good cause. I know some of the guys drop at least ten thousand in a weekend entertaining Vegas showgirls."

Belinda Rice came over to join them, and Chandra made the introductions. Her sister looked wonderful. Her bare face radiated good health. She and Chandra claimed the same eyes and thick dark hair. She then introduced Preston to her parents, nieces, Myles and Zabrina. It was Myles's turn when he introduced her to her nephew for the first time.

It was apparent married life agreed with her brother. His face was fuller than it'd been in years, and the nervous energy that was always so apparent was missing. She'd missed his wedding, but sent a sculpture of a Mayan deity she'd purchased from a local Belizean artisan.

Her anger with Zabrina Mixon for breaking up with Myles two weeks before their wedding had jeopardized her relationship with her brother because he refused to blame Zabrina. What no one knew at the time was that Zabrina was pressured into breaking up with Myles and that she was pregnant with his son.

Myles dropped a proprietary arm around his son's shoulders. "Adam, this lady is your Aunt Chandra. She's been away teaching in Central America. Chandra, this is Adam."

She smiled at the tall, lanky boy who'd inherited his mother's hair and eyes. "Will it be okay if I hug you?" At ten, she wasn't certain whether boys were open to women hugging them. Her question was answered when he stepped forward and put his arms around her waist.

"It's nice meeting you," he said softly.

Chandra squeezed him gently, then lowered her arms. "I've waited a long time for a nephew. You're perfect."

Reaching into her tote, she pulled out an envelope with his name written on the front. "I missed your birthday, so this is a little late. Your dad told me you like to draw, so what's in that envelope should help you buy some art supplies. Or, you can put it into a college fund."

Turning to Zabrina, she extended her arms and wasn't disappointed when the attractive woman with the golden skin, black wavy hair and hazel eyes moved into the circle of her embrace. "Congratulations, Brina. It's a little late, but I want to welcome you into the family."

Zabrina Eaton kissed Chandra's cheek. "Thank you. It's been a long time coming, but in the end everything worked out. Once we finish renovating and decorating the house, Myles and I would love to have you come and spend some time with us."

"Trust me, I will."

Her brother had called to tell her that not only was he marrying Zabrina and that he had a ten-year-old son, but he'd bought a house in a Pittsburgh suburb with enough room to have guests stay for an extended period of time. Adam had started classes at a new private school, while Zabrina managed to secure a position in a nearby public school. His own teaching schedule at Duquesne University School of Law had increased, but he'd managed to balance his professional and personal life, giving each equal attention.

"We'll talk later," she said to Zabrina, repeating what she'd told Denise. Chandra wanted to congratulate her nieces and give them their birthday gifts.

Their heads close together, the girls sat on a webbed lounge chair unwrapping Preston's gifts. Both screamed hysterically when they realized he'd given each of them an iPod touch. They scrambled off the chair and did the happy dance.

Layla whirled like a dervish, her braided hair whipping around her face. "It can hold up to seven thousand songs!"

"We can listen to music and watch movies on it!" Sabrina shrieked excitedly. She executed a dance step where she dropped, popped and locked it.

All of the Eatons exchanged amused glances. Sabrina, the more reserved of the two, had shocked everyone with her effusive enthusiasm.

"Very nice," Chandra whispered to Preston. "How am I going to top that?"

She'd just encountered the same problem as Belinda whenever Griffin gave their nieces and goddaughters more expensive gifts than hers. The unspoken competition continued until they'd become their legal guardians. Becoming parents was very different from being aunt and uncle, and they conferred with each other on every phase of child rearing.

"I'm not competing with you, Chandra," Preston said softly. "When you told me your nieces were turning thirteen, I asked my sister what they would like. I took a chance when I bought the iPod because they could've already had one. And, if they had, then they could take them back to the store and either get a full refund or exchange them for something else. By the way, what did you get them?"

"Electronic readers."

"You're kidding?"

"No, P.J., I'm not kidding. Why?"

"I want one of those."

"Maybe I'll get you one for your birthday."

Preston shook his head. "It passed."

"When was your birthday?"

"March seventeenth. Don't say it. My mother was going to name me Patrick, but changed her mind."

"Maybe I'll get you one for Christmas," Chandra said.

"That'll work. When's your birthday?"

"April twenty-second."

"It's too late to get you something for your birthday, so Christmas will have to do. What do you want for Christmas?"

"Nothing, Preston."

"You're kidding."

Chandra gave him a warm smile. "No, I'm not. I have everything I could ever want."

The minute the admission was out of her mouth she knew she hadn't told the truth. If life could be rewound like a video, then she would've prevented her sister and brother-in-law from getting into their car the day a drunk driver killed them in a head-on collision. But, because life moved forward, not backward, she was grateful that she had her parents, brother, sister and extended family.

Sabrina and Layla screamed again when they opened Chandra's envelope to find gift cards for e-readers and books. Their celebration of becoming teenagers set the tone for an afternoon of casual frivolity. By the time their paternal grandparents, Lucas and Gloria Rice, arrived it was time to sit down and eat. The adults sat at the long table, while Adam, Layla and Sabrina sat at the smaller table. Chandra found herself flanked by Denise and Zabrina. Gloria Rice brought a platter of her celebrated Dungeness crab pot stickers for appetizers, and Roberta Eaton her homemade coconut cake for dessert.

Belinda and Griffin had prepared a smorgasbord of

grilled meat and accompanying sides. There were the ubiquitous spareribs, chicken, pulled pork, roasted corn, fried catfish and hush puppies, carrot slaw, slow-smoked brisket, potato salad and baked beans.

Denise pressed her shoulder to her cousin's. "I didn't expect you to come with *him*," she said sotto voce.

Chandra peered through her lashes at Preston. He sat opposite her with Xavier on his left and Roberta Eaton on his right. "I asked him to come along because he wants to discuss business with Griffin."

Denise speared a portion of carrot slaw. "So, you two are not involved."

Cutting into a slice of smoked barbecue brisket, Chandra popped a piece into her mouth, chewing thoughtfully before she deigned to answer Denise's question. "We're not involved the way you think."

"And why not?" Denise's sultry voice had dropped an octave.

"Firstly, I just met him. And, secondly, I think getting involved would make working together more difficult. I need to remain objective when it comes to a professional relationship."

"Is he paying you?"

"No."

"Then it's not professional, Chandra," Denise argued quietly. "And what's up with the kiss? You guys hardly looked professional with your lips locked together."

Chandra picked up her wineglass and took a swallow. She didn't want to argue with her cousin, especially not in front of others. Although two years younger, Denise had always wanted to tell Chandra what she should or shouldn't do. Rather than go on and on about an issue where they'd never agree, she'd developed the practice of tuning her out.

"If you're interested in Preston, then go for it, Denise." She knew she'd shocked the director of a child care center when her mouth opened, but nothing came out except the sound of her breathing.

"He doesn't want me," Denise said between clenched teeth. "Don't look now, but he's not looking but lusting at you, Chandra. I've been without a man longer than you, so if you get the opportunity to sleep with someone you like, then take it."

Chandra went completely still. "Aren't you seeing Trey Chambers?"

"No!" Everyone at the table turned to stare at Denise, who managed to look embarrassed at her outburst. "I'm sorry about that." She pressed her shoulder to Chandra's. "Bite your tongue, cousin. You know how I feel about Trey. If I wasn't afraid of going to prison for the rest of my life, I'd murder the lying bastard."

"Then why did my mother send me a newspaper article with a photo of the two of you together?"

A frown settled onto Denise's features, distorting her natural beauty. "We serve on some of the same boards. If we're photographed together, then it's only for a photo-op. Trey Chambers ruined my life when I lost the only man I've ever loved."

Chandra heard the wistfulness in Denise's voice. "Have you run into Rhett Fennell now that you live in D.C.?"

Denise shook her head, then put her wineglass to her mouth and drained it. "No. And I pray I don't. I know I would lose it completely if I saw him again. It's been six years, Chandra, and I still can't forget him."

"Snap out of it, Denise Amaris Eaton! You're beautiful, smart, and you're the executive director of one of the most progressive child care centers in the country.

And I know men are making themselves available to you. Meanwhile you're pining after someone you can't have."

"That's so cruel, Chandra."

Resting an arm over Denise's shoulders, Chandra rested her head on her cousin's. "It's the truth and you know it. When you told me that Laurence was only using me, that although he'd put a ring on my finger you couldn't see me spending the rest of my life with him, I said you were cruel and jealous. But you were spot-on with your observation and assessment of our relationship.

"Necie, you're my cousin. I love you and I want you to be happy. I've lost a student to suicide, sister and brother-in-law to a car accident and a man I loved because he wasn't man enough to stand up to his parents. As far as I'm concerned that's more than enough loss in my thirty years of living. If love comes knocking, then I'm going to open the door and grab it, lip-lock it and hold on so tight it would take the Jaws of Life to pry us apart."

"Either you're blind, or you're in denial," Denise drawled. "What you want and need is sitting across the table as we speak. Don't blow it, Chandra. Remember Grandma Eaton's advice about opportunity? She said it's like a bald-headed man. You have to catch him while he's coming toward you, because if your hand slips off then it's over."

Chandra gave Preston a long, penetrating stare. *"Do you think I'll ever be your boyfriend?"* His query came back with vivid clarity. He wanted more and she wanted more, but only he wasn't afraid to verbalize it. An expression of relief swept over her face. Denise had helped her resolve her own dilemma where it concerned Preston Tucker. She would take their grandmother's advice and grasp the opportunity to love before it slipped past her.

Pillars, votives and floodlights lit up the backyard as the Eaton and Rice clan settled down to relax after eating copious amounts of food. The sun had set, taking with it the heat, and a cool breeze swept over those sitting on the patio.

Chandra and Zabrina helped Belinda put away food, while Griffin cleaned up the outdoor kitchen. Griffin's parents, although divorced, had remained friends. They left after dinner because Gloria had tickets to attend a breakfast fundraiser at a local chapter of the NAACP. Myles and his family and the elder Eatons planned to stay overnight with Griffin and Belinda.

The young adults sat off in a corner playing board games, while their parents, grandparents, aunt and uncle lay sprawled on loungers talking quietly to the one closest to them. Leaning back on her palms, Chandra splashed her bare feet in the warm pool water. Preston sat beside her, arms clasped around his knees, flexing his bare feet.

"I talked to Griffin."

She stared at his distinctive profile. "What did he say?"

Preston swung his head around to look at Chandra. "He's agreed to represent me." He winked at her. "I owe you, C.E."

"No, you don't, P.J."

"Yes, I do," he crooned. "I'll have to think of something to show my gratitude."

"I'll take a thank-you."

"I will thank you—but in my own way."

Her gaze dropped to his mouth, lingering on the tuft

of hair under his lip. "Are you going to give me a hint of what I can expect?"

"No. I want it to be a surprise. Let me know when you're ready to leave."

Chandra withdrew her feet from the water. "I'm ready whenever you are." Pushing to his feet, Preston reached down and pulled her up. They had to drive back to Philadelphia before heading to Kennett Square.

She walked over to her parents, leaning over to give each a kiss. "We're leaving now."

Roberta placed a hand alongside her daughter's cheek. "Get home safely. Dwight and I like your young man."

She wanted to tell Roberta that Preston wasn't her young man. He was her friend. "I like him, too, Mama."

"I'll like him as long as he's good to my baby girl," Dwight drawled, deadpan.

"Daddy!"

Roberta swiped at her husband. "Stop teasing the child."

I'm not a child, Chandra mused. She supposed it was hard for family members not to regard her as the baby of the family, when in reality she'd been the most adventuresome.

"Good night," she said in singsong.

Chandra said her goodbyes, promising Denise she would drive down to D.C. to spend time with her, then hugged and kissed her brother and Zabrina, then Xavier. Belinda and Griffin walked her and Preston to the car, lingering long enough to program dates into their cell phones when they would get together again.

"If you guys want a night on the town, then you can

stay over at my place in the city. You can bring your daughters and I'll arrange for a sitter to watch them."

"They can always stay with my parents," Belinda suggested.

"Or my mother," Griffin added.

Chandra smiled. "I guess that means we'll have grown-folk night."

Belinda rested her head on Griffin's shoulder. "We're going to have to get in as many grown-folk outings we can before the baby comes."

"What baby?" Chandra asked, her eyes narrowing.

Griffin smiled at his wife. "We found out yesterday that we're going to have a baby. Lindy and I decided not to say anything until the family gets together again for Thanksgiving. We're telling you, because we want you to be godmother to our son or daughter."

Chandra pantomimed zipping her lips. "I won't say anything, and I'm honored that you've asked me to be godmother." Now she knew why Belinda hadn't drunk anything alcoholic with her meal. "Congratulations to both of you."

After another round of hugs and kisses, Preston assisted Chandra as she slipped into the car. He got in beside her, started the engine, then maneuvered away from the curb, driving down a quiet street-lined street.

He glanced over at Chandra to discover she'd closed her eyes, her chest rising and falling in a measured rhythm. She'd fallen asleep. He would let her sleep until they reached Philadelphia. Once there, he would retrieve his car from the garage. It would be midnight, barring traffic delays, before they reached Kennett Square.

Chapter 9

Chandra didn't know what to expect when Preston said he had a place in the country. But it certainly was not the sprawling stone farmhouse that reminded her of the English countryside. When she got out of Preston's SUV, she half expected to see grazing sheep.

She stood on the front steps leading to the one-story home, staring out into the autumn night. A near-full moon silvered the countryside. "How long have you lived here?"

Preston moved closer, pulling her against his length. "I moved in six years ago. I used to drive through the Brandywine Valley after I got my driver's license, telling myself if I studied and worked hard I would be able to buy property here."

"Your dream came true." Chandra's voice was soft and filled with a strange longing she couldn't disguise.

Preston pressed his mouth to her hair. "What about you? What do you dream about?"

She closed her eyes, enjoying the sensation that came from the solid body molded to hers. How could she tell Preston of her dreams—dreams that were so erotic that when she woke she could still feel the aftermath of a climax, leaving her completely sated.

After the first few dreams Chandra had told herself she was going through withdrawal, and that her body craved the physical fulfillment she'd had with Laurence. But when the dreams continued she realized something else had triggered them—something more than a physical need. If she'd been in the States, there was no doubt she would've sought out a professional therapist to identify the reason why her dreams were solely erotic in nature. They'd gone beyond filling a sexual void. They had become a sexual obsession.

"My dreams aren't the same as a wish list."

"Can you tell me what's on your wish list?"

Peering up at Preston over her shoulder, Chandra tried making out his expression in the moonlight. Only half his face was visible, and there was something about how the shadows struck his features that reminded her of book covers on paranormal novels. They weren't Preston and Chandra in present Pennsylvania, but Pascual and Josette in early nineteenth-century New Orleans, where he'd come to her under the cover of darkness to make the most incredible love imaginable. The fleeting image of Preston making love to her was one she wanted to be real.

Discussing Preston with Denise had helped her rethink her relationship with him. They were friends *and* were collaborating on writing a play, yet there was sexual attraction that was palpable whenever they shared the same space. Preston was brilliant, gorgeous and inexorably male. He was perfect. Almost too perfect, and it was the perfection that gave her pause.

"There's only one thing on Chandra Eaton's wish list," she admitted. "And that is to do whatever makes her feel happy and complete."

Preston stared at the delicate face with eyes that appeared much too wise for someone as young as Chandra. There were times when she stared at him that made him feel as if she knew what he was thinking. Much to his chagrin, most of his thoughts toward her were purely erotic in nature. It was then he chided himself for reading her journal. Perhaps if they'd met on equal footing, then it would've given him the opportunity to look past what she'd written.

He'd tried to separate Chandra from the woman who'd written about her dreams, but he couldn't. There was so much about the woman in his embrace and the one who'd used her imagination to conjure up the most exquisite lover that they were inseparable. What had shocked Preston was that, although each dream was about making love, she'd approached each one differently. It was as if she'd had a different lover every night.

"Are you happy, Chandra?"

The seconds ticked. "I'm at peace, Preston. I don't feel the need to run away to try and find myself. I've come home and I know this time I'll stay."

Chandra had talked to Belinda about buying the furniture in her house, and after a good-natured back-and-forth Belinda agreed to accept a price well below what the pieces were worth. Chandra had been adamant when she refused to accept the bedroom, living room and kitchen furniture as a housewarming gift.

"I'm thirty years old, and for the first time in my life I know and like who I am. And it's taken me this long to accept that I don't need a man in my life to make me complete."

"Don't you want to get married and start a family like your sister?"

Preston knew he had crossed the line with the question, yet he had to know where Chandra stood on the issue if he found himself in too deep. He didn't know what there was about her, but after spending the afternoon with the Eatons it was as if he'd been struck by a bolt of lightning.

He wanted what they had. He wanted to get together with his mother, his sister and her family, but also for a brief instant he'd imagined having his own wife and children. The Eatons and Rices were representative of most families. They loved one another, but also had their disagreements. What he'd noticed was a fierce loyalty that had extended to the next generation. Layla and Sabrina were as protective of Adam as Griffin was of Belinda.

Chandra pondered Preston's query. There was a time when she'd planned to marry and hopefully have children, yet that dream had ended when Laurence bowed to pressure from his overbearing parents to end their engagement.

"I suppose I do."

"Either you do or you don't, Chandra."

She stared at the beam of headlights from a car in the distance maneuvering around a winding road in the valley below. "I do. But it can't be now."

"Why?"

"I have too many things to do. I'm planning to

move into my own place before the beginning of November."

Preston felt a momentary panic. "Where are you moving to?"

"I'm subletting my cousin's Penn's Landing co-op."

He exhaled a breath. He'd thought she was moving out of the state. "That's a nice neighborhood."

"So is Rittenhouse Square," Chandra countered.

"I was looking for something in Society Hill, but there was nothing on the market at the time."

"For someone who appears so contemporary, why do you like old neighborhoods?"

Preston chuckled softly. "There's a certain character in older neighborhoods that I find missing in the ones where all of the buildings are designed like boxes and rectangles. Whether it's the buildings' facades, cobblestone streets or century-old trees, in the historic districts they all have a story to tell. The ones that don't elect to keep their secrets."

Chandra laughed, the rich sound fading in the eerie stillness of the night. "Spoken like a true writer."

Preston's fingers grazed the column of Chandra's neck. "As much as I would love to hang out here with you, we need to go inside and talk about *Death's Kiss*."

"I'd like to take a shower and change into something more comfortable."

"I'll show you to your bedroom, then I'll bring your bag in." Preston had waited in the Eatons' living room while Chandra had gone upstairs to pack a bag. She'd told him that her parents had recently celebrated their forty-second wedding anniversary, and he wondered if his father hadn't died so young whether his parents would've stayed together.

He unlocked the door and walked into the entryway and was met with the subtle scent of fresh roses. The cleaning woman made it a practice of cutting flowers from the garden and arranging them in vases for the entryway and living room.

The flower garden, fireplaces and the house overlooking a valley were what prompted him to purchase the property. The fieldstone house sat on two acres with a copse of trees that provided shade and plenty of firewood. He'd purchased the house several months before he'd proposed marriage to Elaine. His enthusiasm for living in the Brandywine Valley was completely lost on her. She was a city girl who loved living in the city.

"Who arranged the flowers?"

Preston glanced over his shoulder to find Chandra staring at the lush bouquet of late-blooming roses ranging in hues from snow-white to deep purple in a crystal vase resting on a bleached-pine table.

"The woman who comes to dust and vacuum picks them from the garden." The mother of two, who'd come to him asking to clean his house to supplement her income after her husband ran away with his much-younger secretary, had worked for a florist as a teenager, where she'd learned the art of flower arranging.

"You have a flower garden?"

Reaching for Chandra's hand, Preston brought it to his mouth, dropping a kiss on her knuckle before tucking it into the crook of his elbow. "You'll be able to see it tomorrow morning."

"It's already tomorrow," Chandra reminded him with a sly smile.

"And don't tell me you're Cinderella, and at the stroke of midnight you turn back into a chambermaid."

She rolled her eyes upward. "Never happen."

"Did you ever pretend you were a princess when you were a girl?"

"No. My sisters were princesses only because I always insisted on being the queen."

Preston's eyebrows lifted. "They were never the queen?"

"No. I always threw a tantrum and Donna and Belinda knew they had to deal with my father if baby girl came to him crying."

Smiling, he shook his head. "You must have been a hot mess."

Chandra flashed a Cheshire cat grin. "I used whatever I had at my disposal. Being the baby of the family had its disadvantages, and I did whatever was necessary to shift the odds."

"Conniving little wench."

"What…eva," she drawled.

Preston led her into a living room with a massive brick fireplace that opened out to a dining room. If his Rittenhouse Square condo was ultracontemporary, it was the opposite of the farmhouse in the historic Brandywine Valley. A sofa and two facing love seats were upholstered with fabric stamped with flowers, ferns and vines. A coffee table in antique cherry was big enough to double as a place for an informal tea party. Plank cherrywood floors were covered with area rugs that complemented the furnishings. Roses on mochaccino wallpaper and a collection of green crockery and majolica in the dining room evoked the feeling of a Victorian period piece.

"Who decorated your house?" Every piece of furniture and accessories were chosen with the utmost care and consideration.

"My mother."

"She has impeccable taste." Rose Tucker's knowledge of historic preservation was apparent when each item conformed to the design of the updated eighteenth-century farmhouse.

"I'll let her know you said so. This will be your bedroom." Preston stepped aside to let Chandra enter a room with a connecting door to his bedroom. "Mine is through that door." He pointed to a carved mahogany door on the left. "The door on the right is your bathroom."

"Lovely." The single word slipped unbidden between her lips.

Sheltered beneath eaves that reminded her of an attic, Chandra looked at the queen-size bed covered with a quilt pieced with geometric patterns in a mix of plaids, stripes and paisleys. A mound of pillows in soft shades of coffee and cream were nestled against a wrought-iron headboard. An upholstered club chair in a faint brown-and-white pinstripe cradled an off-white chenille throw. She couldn't stop the smile spreading across her face. The charming bedroom had a window seat where one could curl up to read, relax or just stare out the window.

"It reminds me of my bedroom when I was a girl. I grew up in a farmhouse outside Philly," she explained when Preston gave her a questioning look. "My mother never had to go looking for us, because we always played around the house. The best thing about growing up in the suburbs was having a pet. We had dogs, cats, birds, rabbits and baby chicks. But, when the rabbits started multiplying and the chickens grew into hens or roosters, we had to give them away."

Cradling her face, Preston pressed a kiss to Chandra's forehead. "So, you like living in the country?"

She smiled. "I prefer it to the city. Waking up not hearing car horns or sirens from emergency vehicles alleviates more than fifty percent of one's stress. Which do you prefer? The city or the country?"

"The country."

"Why, then, do you have a place in the city?"

"That's where I entertain and conduct business. I plot at the apartment, but this is where I write because of the natural light." He kissed her again. "Let me get your bag. Knock on my door whenever you're ready."

Chandra stood up in the tub, reaching for a fluffy towel on a stack on a nearby stool. She'd lingered in the bathtub longer than she'd planned because soaking in a tub had become not only a luxury but also a privilege. When she'd entered the bathroom she felt as if she'd stepped back in time. Twin pedestal sinks and a slipper tub harkened back to another century.

The clock on a shelf chimed the hour. It was one o'clock. If she hadn't napped in the car during the ride from Paoli to Philly, there was no doubt she wouldn't have been able to keep her eyes open. Patting the moisture from her body, Chandra stepped out onto a thirsty shag bathmat and moisturized her body with a scented crème before retreating to the bedroom and pulling on a pair of black-and-white-striped cotton lounging pants with a white tank top. Walking on bare feet, she knocked lightly on the connecting door.

She knocked again, listening for movement on the other side. "Preston." Waiting a full minute, she knocked again. "Preston, please open the door." Again, there was no answer, and Chandra placed her hand on the doorknob, turning it slowly.

Pushing open the door, she stuck her head in. A

lamp on a bedside table was turned to its lowest setting, casting a soft glow over the expansive space. A smile replaced her expression of uncertainty when she saw Preston sprawled on a king-size bed. He'd changed out of his suit and into a pair of drawstring white cotton pajama pants.

With wide eyes Chandra moved closer to the bed. Preston had fallen asleep while waiting for her. She felt like a voyeur when she was able to brazenly gaze at his toned upper body. Fully clothed, Preston Tucker was captivating; half-clothed he was mesmerizing.

For a man approaching forty who earned a living sitting behind a desk, she hadn't expected a flat belly, defined abdominals and muscled pectorals. She leaned closer, inhaling the lingering scent of soap on his skin, while staring at the tattooed masks of comedy and tragedy over his heart. Without warning his breathing changed, becoming more ragged, but within seconds it resumed its normal cadence. Turning on her heels, Chandra headed toward the door.

"Where are you going?"

She stopped and turned. Preston had sat up and swung his legs over the side of the bed. "I thought you were asleep."

Preston ran a hand over his cropped hair. "I guess I dozed off waiting for you." He beckoned her, then patted the mattress. "Come and sit down. Come, baby. I'm not going to bite you," he urged, sensing her hesitation.

Chandra took a tentative step, then another, before racing to the bed and launching herself at him. He caught her midair, flipped her onto her back, straddling her.

His gaze lingered on the hair she'd twisted into a knot atop her head, then moved leisurely down to her scrubbed face. "What took you so long?"

Her lids lowered, a dreamy expression softening her delicate features. "It's been a while since I've had the luxury of lingering in a bathtub."

"Did you enjoy yourself?"

Chandra smiled. "Immensely."

Burying his face between her chin and shoulder, Preston breathed a kiss against the column of her scented neck. "That's good."

The heat, the comforting crush of Preston's body and the increasing hardness between his thighs enveloped Chandra as she struggled valiantly not to succumb to the familiar sensations of rising desire. She hadn't been dreaming, or if she had she hadn't remembered, since her return. What she felt was beginning to remind her of the dreams she'd recorded in her journals.

"Preston?"

He groaned in her ear. "What, baby?"

Chandra struggled not to move her hips. "We're supposed to be talking, not making love."

"We're not making love, Chandra."

She closed her eyes when she felt the outline of his erection against her thigh, while the intense heat from his body threatened to swallow her whole. In a motion so quick it caused her to catch her breath, he reversed their positions, she lying between his outstretched legs.

"Preston?"

"What is it, baby?"

"What exactly are we doing?"

Cradling the back of her head in one hand, Preston rested his other one over her rounded bottom. "We're going to talk about Pascual and Josette."

Chandra wanted to tell Preston that she loved it when he called her baby. It came out in a sensual growl. "What about them?"

"Stop wiggling, or my hard-on will never go down."

Chandra's head popped up, her eyes meeting Preston's. "I was trying to get into a more comfortable position."

"And I'm trying not to spend the rest of the night in pain."

A frown creased her smooth forehead. "Why would you be in pain?"

The seconds ticked as Preston gave her an incredulous look. "Are you a virgin?"

Stunned by his bluntness, her mouth opened, snapped closed, then opened again. "No!"

"No!" he repeated. "If you're familiar with the male anatomy, then you should know men can't sustain an erection for an extended time without a release because it hurts like hell."

"I know that."

"If you know that, then stop teasing me."

Chandra tried to sit up; her efforts were thwarted when Preston held her fast. "Let me go, Preston."

He tightened his hold around her waist. "Now, you know I can't do that, baby. Do you know how hard it's been for me to keep my hands off you?"

"No," she answered truthfully.

"Well, it has. I never imagined how much my life would change when I found your journal in that taxi. My first impulse was to give it to the driver, but I changed my mind."

"So, you opened it and saw my contact information in my journal."

"Yes. And I'm glad I did."

"Do you actually think I believe you were just waiting to meet some anonymous woman?"

Preston glared at Chandra. There were times when

he wanted to shake her. He didn't know why she was distrustful. "What the hell did your last boyfriend do to you?"

Chandra averted her gaze while chewing her lower lip. Once she'd gathered her family together to inform them she wasn't marrying Laurence, it was the last time she'd mentioned his name. She'd convinced herself that if she didn't have to retell the story of what went wrong then she wouldn't have to reopen a wound that took years to heal.

"I'd rather not talk about it," she said after a pregnant pause.

"Not talking about it won't make it any less painful."

Her gaze shifted back to Preston as her lips thinned in anger. "There's no pain, Preston, just rage whenever I think about it. The funny thing is that I don't blame Laurence as much as I do his parents. We dated for a year before he asked me to marry him. I accepted, and then the next step was meeting his mother and father, who were quick to tell me I was so wrong for their precious baby boy."

"What do you mean by *wrong?*"

"I didn't have the right *pedigree.*" She spat out the word.

Eyes narrowing, Preston angled his head. Instinctually, he knew it had to go beyond pedigree. The Eatons were one of Philadelphia's prominent African-American families. "You didn't have the right pedigree or the right color?"

The breath caught in Chandra's lungs. "How did you know?"

Preston gave her a look usually reserved for children. "Chandra, please don't insult my intelligence. It was their politically correct way of saying they didn't want their son to marry a black woman. If they had wanted to have you investigated, then the P.I. would've told them that you come from a family of doctors, teachers and lawyers, so it had to be something else. And for me, race was the only other obvious variable."

She shook her head. "I don't know why I didn't think of that."

"It was because you were young and very much in love with someone who didn't deserve your love. If you give me his address I'll pay him a visit."

A frown formed between her eyes. "And do what, Preston?"

"Kick his ass, of course."

"You wouldn't?"

"Hell, yeah. I can promise you he wouldn't look the same after I give him an old-fashion North Philly beat down."

"Don't tell me there's some thug in Philadelphia's famed dramatist."

Preston glared at her under lowered brows. "There's a lot of thug in me. However, I'm able to channel most of it into writing."

"The only time I got a little feisty is when Laurence's mother said it was nothing personal, but she had expected her son would marry someone within his social circle. I told her I understood exactly what she was saying because as a Thoroughbred I should've never hooked up with a jackass."

Throwing back his head, Preston howled, Chandra's laughter joining his as tears ran down their cheeks. She rolled off his body to lie beside him. "I'm glad it turned out the way it did, otherwise I never would've met you."

"Is that a good thing, P.J.?"

He closed his eyes. "It's a very good thing, C.E."
Turning on his side, he rested an arm over her belly.
"The Tuckers' pedigree can't begin to match the Eatons',
but I'd like to hope that I at least have a chance to prove
to you that I'm not a jackass."

Chandra shifted, facing Preston, their faces only
inches apart. She studied the features of the man who'd
managed to scale the wall she'd erected around her in
order to protect herself from heartbreak.

She knew he wanted to make love to her, and she
wanted to make love with him. Unknowingly, he'd
become the nameless, faceless man who'd invaded her
sleep and dreams to assuage her sexual frustration.

"You could never be a jackass," Chandra whispered
against his parted lips. She tasted his mouth tentatively
as if sampling a frothy confection.

Nothing on Preston moved, not even his eyes as he
relished her caress of his mouth. "What do you want,
Chandra?"

"I want you," she said.

"How?"

The kisses stopped, and she stared at him. "I want
you to make love with me."

Preston smiled. She hadn't asked him to make love
to her, but with her. His right eyebrow lifted a fraction
before settling back into place. "And I want you to make
love with me." He pressed a kiss over each eye. "Are
you using birth control?"

Pinpoints of heat dotted Chandra's cheeks. In her
dreams she hadn't had to worry about conception; but
the man in whose bed she lay wasn't a specter or figment
of her imagination but flesh and blood and capable of
getting her pregnant.

"No."

Preston kissed her again. "I will protect you." And he would. He would protect her from an unplanned pregnancy and protect her from anything and anyone seeking to harm her. It was in that instant that he realized he was falling in love with Chandra Eaton.

Chapter 10

Chandra stared at the flexing muscles in Preston's abdomen when he sat up and swung his legs over the side of the bed. She was certain he could hear the runaway beating of her heart as he opened the drawer in the bedside table. She exhaled a ragged, audible sigh when he placed a condom on the pillow beside her head. It was one thing to sleep with a man she'd known a very short time and another to find herself pregnant with his child.

Her relationship with Preston differed greatly from the ones her sister and brother had with their respective spouses. Belinda had been maid of honor and Griffin best man at their siblings' wedding, and Myles had known Zabrina all his life before finally marrying her last month, while she was preparing to sleep with a man she hadn't met two weeks before.

Preston stood up, untied the cord to his pajama pants,

letting them slide off his waist and hips. His gaze met and fused with Chandra's when he stepped out of them. Her breath quickened. The blood pooled in his groin when he noticed the outline of her hardened nipples against the white tank top.

He stared at her, wanting to commit to memory the cloud of dark curly hair around her face, breasts that were fuller than he'd expected and the look of indecision in the eyes staring back at him in anxious anticipation.

The mattress dipped slightly when he placed one knee, then the other on the bed. Lying beside Chandra, Preston turned to face her. "How are you?"

A tentative smile trembled over her lips. "I'm good, Preston."

He ran the back of his hand over her cheek. "Are you ready for this? If not, then we can sleep together without making love."

Shifting slightly, Chandra draped her leg over his. "I'm ready."

She was more than ready. Preston hadn't even touched her intimately, yet she could feel the trickle of desire coursing through her body.

Preston rose slightly to grasp the hem of Chandra's top, easing it up and over her head. He took his time undressing her, because he had all night in which to make her dreams real. Reading her journal gave him an advantage: he knew what she liked. Ironically, what she liked, he liked, and then some.

He untied her lounging slacks, easing them down her hips. A wide smile split his face when he saw the tiny triangle of black silk covering her mound. Lowering his head, he nibbled at the bows holding up her thong panty. Chandra arched off the bed, and he placed a hand over her belly, preventing her from escaping his marauding mouth.

She'd teased him about his mouth and his ability to kiss and he'd interpreted it as a challenge. He'd become an overachiever because of his father's taunts when he'd revealed he wanted to become a writer. When Craig Tucker told his son he would end up a pauper, Preston had set out to prove his father wrong. Unfortunately, Craig hadn't lived long enough to witness his son's success.

Chandra covered her face with both hands when Preston's moist hot breath seared the apex of her thighs much like the heat from a blast furnace. Delicious spasms made the sensitive flesh of her sex quiver. A rush of moisture bathed her core. In the past it had taken prolonged foreplay to arouse her.

She teased Preston about what he could with his mouth, but that mouth was doing unbelievable things to her. He'd alternated kissing and licking her cropped pubic mound. Without warning, tears flooded her eyes and spilled down her face. His tongue found the swollen bud between the folds. He licked it in an up-and-down motion that made her rise off the mattress.

"No more, Preston. Please stop."

Preston heard her plaintive cry. He would stop, but not before he tasted every inch of her fragrant body. Moving up between her legs, he claimed her mouth in an explosive kiss, his tongue plunging into her mouth.

Everything about Chandra Eaton was intoxicating: her smell, the perfection of her firm breasts, the curvy fullness of her hips, the narrow waist he could span with both hands and the taste of her sex. Her body was a banquet table where he wanted to feast again and again.

With the precision of a cartographer, he charted a course beginning with her mouth, journeying downward to her bared throat, the column of her scented neck and lower to her breasts. He suckled her like a starving infant, and when drinking his fill he worried the erect nipples with his teeth. The keening coming from Chandra made tiny shivers of gooseflesh on the back of his neck.

Chandra was lost in a web of pleasure so sensual, so wholly erotic that she felt as if she were slipping away to nothingness. Preston's mouth and hands seemed to be everywhere at once.

Preston heard and felt Chandra's breathing quicken, and he knew she was ready to climax. He released her long enough to slip on the condom, then moved between her legs once again. Reaching for her hand, he placed it on his erection.

He kissed her neck. "Let's do this together."

Preston had asked Chandra if she was a virgin, and at that moment she felt like one. In each relationship she'd let her partner take the lead, yet it was different with Preston. They had become equals—in and out of bed.

Her fingers closed around his heavy sex, then Preston's hand covered hers as he positioned his erection at the entrance to her vagina. She gasped slightly as the penetration seemingly took minutes to complete. They shared a smile and a sigh when he was fully sheathed inside her.

Preston did not want to believe the incredible heat that came from Chandra. He wanted to withdraw and pull off the condom just to experience flesh against flesh, heat on heat. Not only was she tight, but she was on fire.

"Oh, baby, I—" Chandra silenced him with a searing kiss that scorched his mouth with its intensity when her teeth sank into his lip. Her hips moved against his, and he was lost.

Her hunger and need was transferred to Preston and he answered. He moved slowly, deliberately. Each time he pulled back it was a little farther, and each time he pushed it was a little harder and deeper.

Chandra's wrapping her legs around Preston's waist was his undoing. Sliding his hands under her hips, he lifted her off the mattress, permitting him deeper penetration. Moans and groans escalated, breathing quickened, then the dam broke. Burying his face against her neck, Preston exploded, his deep moans of ecstasy echoing in her ear.

He's real. What I'm feeling is real. Chandra had waited more than three years to experience why she'd been born female. The flutters that began with his penetration grew stronger. Her muscles contracted around his rigid flesh, pulling him in, holding him fast; she released him before squeezing him again and again.

The walls of her vagina convulsed as a scorching climax hurtled her to a place where she'd never been. Preston Japheth Tucker was the only man she'd slept with able to bring her to climax their first time together.

"I think I'm going to keep you, P.J."

Preston chuckled. "You better, because I don't intend to let you go." He brushed a kiss over her cheek. "I'm going to have to get up." She emitted a small cry of protest when he pulled out.

He left the bed and walked to the bathroom, where he discarded the condom and washed away the evidence of their lovemaking. He'd tried imagining what it would be like to make love to Chandra, but nothing in his imagination could've prepared him for the passion she stirred up in him.

Preston returned to the bedroom to find it shrouded in darkness. Chandra had turned off the lamp. He managed to make it to the bed without bumping into anything. Slipping into bed, he pulled her against his chest. "Are you okay?"

"Yes-s-s," Chandra slurred.

"Do you want to talk about Pascual and Josette?"

"Not now."

"When?"

"Tomorrow morning."

Preston wanted to remind Chandra it was already tomorrow. They had tomorrow and hopefully many more tomorrows.

Ribbons of sunlight from the partially closed drapes threaded their way over the bed where Preston lay, his back to Chandra. He opened his eyes, staring at the door connecting the two bedrooms. A smile softened his mouth when he recalled what he'd shared with Chandra Eaton.

He didn't know why he'd been the one to get into the taxi where she'd left her case, or what had prompted him to read her journal. Whether it was a fluke, serendipity or destiny, he regarded it as a blessing.

He and his younger sister had grown up in a neighborhood where muggings, the sound of gunfire and a heavy police presence were the norm. Some of his boyhood friends never reached adulthood, or if they did then they'd become a statistic in the criminal justice system.

Preston had lost count of the number of times his

mother and father preached to him and Yolanda about making something of their lives. The first and only time Craig Tucker asked his son what he wanted to be when he grew up and was told a writer, it elicited a long tirade about how writers were born not made, and very few, if any, earn enough money to support themselves and their families.

Although Craig had passed away years before he walked into Princeton for his first day of classes, Preston couldn't shake off his father's dire warning. Praying his late father was wrong, he majored in English with a minor in mathematics. His rationale was if he couldn't make it as a writer he could always teach math. But he'd proven Craig wrong on two accounts: he hadn't become a victim of the streets, and he *hadn't* failed as a writer.

"Will you share my bath with me?"

Preston's smile grew wider. Hearing Chandra's voice, still heavy with sleep, was the perfect way for him to start his day. He swallowed a groan. She'd pressed her firm breasts against his back.

"What do I get if I say yes?"

"I'll wash your back and any place or anything else you want."

This time Preston couldn't stop the groan escaping his parted lips when his sex hardened with her erotic offer. He curbed the urge to reach between his thighs. He scrambled off the bed and practically ran to the en suite bathroom.

Chandra waited for Preston to return, but when he didn't she left the bed and walked into her bathroom. She turned on the faucets in the bathtub, adjusting the water temperature before adding a capful of scented bath crystals under the flowing water. The tub was half-filled by the time she'd washed her face and brushed her teeth.

She let out an audible sigh when sinking into the lukewarm water. The slight ache between her legs was a reminder of what she'd shared with the man who was now a part of her life as she was his.

What had begun with him returning her case and journal was now a full-blown affair. Resting her arms on the sides of the tub, Chandra closed her eyes and smiled. She was having an affair with P. J. Tucker.

How, she mused, had her life changed in a matter of weeks? She'd had her first sexual encounter during her college sophomore year. He was another student in her study group, and she'd slept with him not because she was in love with him. If the truth were told, then she would have to admit that she barely *liked* him. She'd gone to his apartment to study for a statistics exam, and was forced to spend the night when a winter storm dropped a foot of snow on New York City. She slept with him again a week later, then decided they were better off as friends than lovers.

Then there was Laurence, whom she dated for six months before getting into bed with him. Although she'd found sex with him satisfying, it wasn't exciting. After a while she was resigned to the fact she would marry a man who would provide financial stability for her and their children and do whatever he could to make their marriage a success.

Laurence Breslin may have been what Chandra thought of as benign, but she hadn't been prepared for his reversal of affection. He'd professed she was the love of his life, yet when confronted by *Mommy* he folded like an accordion and sided with his parents against her.

"Do you intend to keep your promise to wash my back?"

She opened her eyes to find Preston lounging against the door frame, arms crossed over his bare chest. He'd put on the pajama pants he'd discarded the night before. Her gaze moved slowly over the stubble on his lean jaw, down to his magnificent upper body, long legs and bare, arched feet.

Sinking lower in the tub, Chandra winked at Preston. "Yes. I always keep my promises."

Lowering his arms, Preston approached the tub, at the same time pushing the pajamas down his hips. It had taken months before his mother was able to locate a slipper tub large enough for two adults. He'd used it once, but preferred taking a shower. It was his sister who used it whenever she came for a visit.

"Scoot forward, baby." Chandra inched toward the opposite end of the tub, and he got in behind her. Scooping up a handful of warm scented water, he poured it over her shoulders. "You know I'm going to smell like a girl," Preston whispered in her ear.

Resting the back of her head on his shoulder, Chandra smiled up at Preston. "There are worse things you could smell like."

His eyebrows lifted. "True. It's a good thing I'm secure about my sexuality or I would be having a few issues."

"I take it you like being a man?"

"Very much. How about you, Chandra? Do you like being a woman?"

"I love being a woman."

Preston's minty breath wafted in her nose. "And what a magnificent woman you are, Chandra Eaton."

Her lids lowered demurely. "Thank you."

"Don't thank me. The thanks go to your parents and their superior gene pool."

"I thought we were going to discuss Josette and Pascual."

"We did, but that was before you distracted me."

Chandra's jaw dropped. "You're blaming me for what happened last night?"

Preston nodded. "If you hadn't come into my bedroom wearing that little skimpy top showing the outline of your nipples—"

"Don't you dare go there, P.J.! You're as much to blame for what took place. Don't," she screamed when his hands cupped her wet breasts, his thumbs sweeping back and forth over her nipples.

"Now, let's talk about Pascual and Josette."

"I can't think with you doing that," Chandra said in protest.

"Is this better?"

She rose several inches when his hand moved from her breast to the area between her thighs. "Preston. If you don't stop, I'm getting out of this tub."

Chandra wanted him to make love to her again, and she also wanted to discuss the play. She didn't know how much more free time she'd have once she began the task of moving into her new residence. Then, there was the possibility that she would be contacted for a substitute or permanent teaching position. Business before pleasure had always been her credo for balancing her life.

Preston didn't have the pressure of looking for a job or a place to live. He owned a condo and a house in the country, while she was subletting from her cousin. She'd saved enough money to sustain her for two years, but only if she continued to live with her parents.

But for Chandra that wasn't an option. She wanted her own place. She wanted to invite whomever she chose to stay over when the mood hit her. Her parents had raised four children, and now that they were in their sixties they could do and go anywhere they chose without having to worry whether their house would be standing when they returned.

Chandra had lived on campus when she attended Columbia, was provided with faculty housing when she taught at the private school in Northern Virginia and during her Peace Corps tenure. She'd celebrated her thirtieth birthday in April, and she still didn't own property or a car.

"Sorry, baby," he apologized, kissing her mussed hair.

She blew Preston an air kiss. "Apology accepted."

Lowering his head, Preston brushed his mouth over hers in a peace offering. "I've plotted the first act of the play."

Settling against his chest, Chandra closed her eyes. "Tell me about it."

Preston wrapped his arms around her waist. "You can interrupt me whenever you need clarification. As I mentioned before, the opening scene will be Josette getting off a ship in New Orleans. She garners a lot of attention not only because she's very beautiful but because she's wearing an Empire-waist gown that is now the rage in Paris."

"Does she look like a woman of color?"

"Her mother, Marie, is mulatto and Josette is a quadroon. Although fair in coloring, she wouldn't be able to pass for white. Her mother meets her at the pier with her household slaves."

Chandra opened her eyes. "Her mother owns slaves?"

"Yes, baby. Many *gens de couleur* owned slaves. Marie, as *placée* to a wealthy Creole planter, would have a personal maid and manservant."

"Please continue, Preston."

"Marie is going on about the upcoming quadroon ball and she has arranged for Josette to become *placée* to the son of the wealthiest man in New Orleans. Marie overrides Josette's protest when she taps her on the hand with her fan. They arrive home and Josette retreats to her room where she writes a letter to a young man she met in Paris. He is also a man of color, but she knows her mother will not permit her to marry an African. In order to hide her liaison from her mother, she addresses the letter to his sister to give to him.

"The next scene is at the shop of a dressmaker where Josette is to be fitted for a ball gown. She spies a man in the latest European fashion lounging on a chair. When their gazes meet, she suddenly finds herself feeling faint. He gets up to assist, but Marie steps in between them to aid her daughter. The shopkeeper revives her with smelling salts, then leads her into a dressing room.

"Josette suffers through being measured and having to select fabric for her dress. When she emerges from the dressing room she sees the strange man with a woman. I've already established that Francesca is Pascual's sister and a vampire who has to feed, whereas Pascual doesn't."

Chandra smiled. "I like that."

Preston inclined his head. "I thought you would. Josette gets to see Pascual again at the flower market. He buys a nosegay, then presents it to her. She is reluctant to accept it, because her mother has lectured her about talking to men to whom she hasn't been formally introduced. But Josette thinks herself more French than American, and the girls with whom she interacted at her school thought of themselves as libertines. A few of them had become mistresses to wealthy men, while others took lovers by their leave. Pascual gives her a card, asking whether he can call on her. She tucks the card into her reticule, then presents him with her back. When Pascual tells her the woman she saw him with was his sister, she tells him he will hear from her."

"Does she contact him?"

"Yes. She sends the maid with a note to Pascual at the boardinghouse where he's living during his stay in the Crescent City. She invites him to share afternoon tea with her and her mother, a ritual she discovered during a visit to London. I haven't fleshed out the scene between the three of them because you have tell me how Pascual supports himself."

"He's a hide exporter. He has turned vast tracts of land into horse and cattle ranches."

"Nice," Preston complimented. "What does he do to pass his time in New Orleans?"

"He does what most men of leisure during that time did—whore, drink and gamble."

Throwing back his head, Preston laughed. "Damn, baby, you didn't have to say it like that."

"Well, it's true."

"You're probably right."

"I am right," Chandra argued softly. "I did the research. Knowing this, will Marie be receptive to him?"

"She's charmed by him because he appears to be a

wealthy foreigner, but she has signed a contract to have Josette become *placée* to an American. Her dilemma is that the contract is as legal and binding as a marriage certificate. If she permits Josette to become involved with Pascual, then she's risking her future because her daughter's father may withdraw his financial support. *Placée* notwithstanding, she cannot insult or embarrass a white man. Pascual shocks Marie when he offers to make Josette his wife, not his mistress or *placée*. Unfortunately, Marie will not concede, and tells him he can find another quadroon if he attends the ball. Pascual has decided he wants Josette. The scene ends when he tells Francesca he will have Josette. He will go as far as ordering Francesca to turn Josette into a vampire."

Chandra applauded, her heart racing with excitement. "Bravo! Bravo! What have you planned for the second act?"

Lacing his fingers together over her belly, Preston pulled Chandra closer. "You and I will have to work closely together on act two."

"Why?"

"This act will be solely about seduction. It will begin with the ball and the Regency dance, which can be the English Country Dance, the Cotillion, Quadrille, waltz and *your* tango. Of course, I'll have to hire a choreographer. Josette's benefactor will be introduced in this act."

"What does he look like?"

Preston paused. "All I'm going to say is, physically he's the complete opposite of Pascual."

"Don't tell me he's blond, short and frail-looking."

Preston nodded.

"No, Preston! The only thing missing is spectacles and he would be a nineteenth-century nerd."

"What do you want, baby?"

"Make him a worthy competitor. He can be blond, but he can also be gorgeous. Also make him a little older. Perhaps early thirties. Compared to Pascual's two hundred-plus years he's a mere baby."

Preston gave her a long, penetrating look. "Okay. Basil, who will be called Bazz-el, will be Pascual's mirror image."

"Don't forget to include a voodoo ritual replete with drums and dancers. I want everyone in the audience to feel as if they'd been transported to the motherland."

Lowering his head, he nipped the side of her neck. "How would you like to take a trip to the motherland with me?"

"What are you talking about, Preston?"

"Let's go back to bed."

Chandra flashed a saucy grin. "And do what, baby?"

"I don't know, baby," he teased. "Perhaps you can show me what to do."

"Stand up, Preston," she ordered. "Come on, darling. Please stand up."

Deciding it was better to humor Chandra than continue to question her, Preston pushed to his feet. He'd regained his footing at the same time she went to her knees, facing him.

"No!" Preston bellowed like a wounded animal when he felt the heat of her mouth on his sex. Chandra had wrapped her arms around his thighs, holding him fast.

He hardened quickly as he stared, stunned, at his penis moving in and out of her mouth. Eyes closed, fists clenched, he succumbed to the most exquisite pleasure he'd ever had in his life.

Bending over, he forcibly extricated her arms, slid down to the cool water and pushed inside her with one, sure thrust. Between sanity and insanity, heaven and hell, he drove into her like a man possessed. Then without warning, he pulled out at the last possible moment, moaning as he spilled his passion in the water.

"You didn't like it?" she asked innocently.

Preston glared at Chandra, his gaze raking her face like talons. "I loved it, Chandra. But you're driving me crazy," he gasped. He should've known what to expect; what had just occurred was ripped from the pages of her journal.

Moisture dotted Chandra's face when she opened her eyes. "That makes two of us. Now, please let me up. I need to take a shower."

He stepped out of the tub, she feeling the heat from his gaze on her wet body as she headed to a corner shower stall. Closing the door, she turned on the water, then slid down to the tiled floor. Her attempt to live out her fantasy with Preston had nearly met with disaster. He'd entered her without a condom during the most fertile time of her cycle. If he hadn't pulled out, then the risk of her becoming pregnant was more than ninety-nine percent.

The door opened; Preston stepped in and closed the door behind him. Anchoring his hands under her shoulders, he eased her to stand. "We can't do that again. Not unless you want a baby."

Water spiked her lashes when Chandra glanced up at Preston. "It won't happen again."

"I want it to happen again," he crooned. "It just can't happen unless I'm wearing protection."

He pulled her to his chest, rocking her from side to side. They stood under the falling water, rinsing the lingering soap from their bodies. Minutes later they stood on a bath mat drying each other's body.

They'd made love—twice, discussed *Death's Kiss* and had to prepare for Ray Hardy and his wife.

Chapter 11

Chandra knew she'd made an error in judgment when she'd initiated oral sex. Although he'd claimed to have liked it, she wasn't certain whether he appreciated her assertive take-charge approach. Although not as sexually experienced as some of her classmates and/ or coworkers—her sum total of liaisons was limited to two—she'd become a participant whenever sex became the topic of conversation. It was those explicit conversations, coupled with pornographic films, that fueled her fertile imagination.

She'd bonded with three single female teachers at Cambridge Valley Prep. When they didn't have dates, they usually got together on either Friday or Saturday nights. If they met in her apartment, then it'd become Chandra's responsibility to provide the food and beverages. In order to avoid a conflict, they'd set up a rotating schedule for their get-togethers.

One night someone rented a pornographic movie, and when the images appeared on the television screen it was to stunned silence. They laughed at most of the antics because the acting was so contrived, but viewing the movie served as a pleasant diversion for their girls' night.

Afterward, they scheduled one day a month as "naughty night." Most times they wound up critiquing the acting, or lack thereof, plot and set decorations.

Chandra pulled on a pair of faded jeans, thick white socks and a cotton sweater with a rolled neckline and cuffs in a soft oatmeal shade. She'd towel-dried her hair, brushed it and pulled it into a ponytail. Preston told her their meeting with the Hardys was casual and informal.

She cleaned up the bathroom, then turned her attention to making the bed.

"I didn't invite you here to do housework."

She turned to see Preston in the doorway, hands folded at his hips. Jeans, a navy blue waffle-weave pullover and running shoes completed his casual look. He'd showered but hadn't shaved.

"I have a thing about unmade beds," she retorted.

"Get over it, Chandra. Now, come eat breakfast."

Chandra didn't move. "Are you pissed with me?"

Preston lowered his hands as his expression stilled, becoming a mask of stone. "What are you talking about?"

"Are you upset because I took the initiative in making love to you?"

Closing the distance between them, Preston stood over her like an avenging angel. "Do you really hear yourself? Did I tell you that I was upset? Do I look upset?"

"I don't know, Preston."

"Well, I'm not. It's not about who initiates what. For me it's about enjoying making love with you. Now if you're talking about unprotected sex, then that's something we can discuss. If I do father a child, then I want it to be by mutual consent. When I asked you whether you want marry or have children, your response was you do, but it can't be now. And to me, that translates into my protecting you."

There was something about the way Preston was looking at her that made Chandra feel as if he could read her mind. "I understand."

"No, you don't understand, baby. You truly have no idea what you are doing to me."

With wide eyes, she asked, "What am I doing to you?"

"You're turning me into a madman. Whenever we're apart I find myself obsessing about you, while trying to come up with any excuse to bring us together. You're beautiful and you're smart. I love the way you smell, how you taste and your feistiness. And I love the fact that you're a tad bit wicked in bed."

Chandra took a step, resting her head on Preston's shoulder. She longed to tell him that she loved everything about him, yet was reluctant because she didn't want a repeat of what she'd had with Laurence. She'd been the first one to bare her soul, confessing that she was in love with him. Only after their breakup did she realize he'd never professed to loving her. He wanted her, adored her, was proud of her, but the dreaded four-letter word was never a part of his verbal repertoire.

"Just a tad?" she whispered in the fabric of his shirt.

Resting his chin on the top of Chandra's head, Preston smiled. "Is there more?"

Easing back, she stared into the velvety dark eyes of the man who made her feel things she didn't want to feel and made her do "naughty" things to him. "There's a lot more."

Attractive lines fanned out around Preston's eyes when his smile grew wider. "I can assure you that you won't get a complaint from me."

"We'll see."

"Should I be afraid of you, C.E.?"

She patted his chest. "No. P.J. I just want you to enjoy it."

"And I promise you, I will." His eyes caressed her face seconds before he grasped her hand and led her out of the bedroom and into the kitchen.

A cool breeze wafted through screens at the quartet of windows spanning one wall. Roberta Eaton claimed that the kitchen was the heart of any home, and judging from Preston's it wasn't only the heart but also its lifeblood. The generously proportioned space combined classic materials with practical up-to-date amenities.

White cabinetry, stainless steel appliances, black granite countertops afforded the kitchen the appearance of those in the grand estates of a bygone era. A third sink fitted in an oversize island was ideal for several cooks to work at the same time.

Her smile was dazzling. "I like it."

Preston dropped a kiss on Chandra's hair. She liked his kitchen and what he felt for her went far beyond a casual liking. He wondered how Chandra would react if she knew he wanted a commitment from her—that they would see each other exclusively.

After he and Elaine mutually decided to go their

separate ways, he'd almost become a serial dater. He'd dated women he liked and the ones he tolerated were there to fill up the empty spaces when he wasn't writing. It took a great deal of soul-searching for him to realize he didn't need to see a different woman every other week, or sleep with a different one every couple of months. Preston knew some of the women wanted more, but he refused to offer more. His work had become a jealous mistress he didn't want to give up.

Whenever he began a new project, he wrote in seclusion, averaging four hours of sleep and eating one meal a day. He'd shower, but wouldn't bother to shave. It was during his marathon writing sessions that he refused all social invitations. With Chandra Eaton he could have both: writing and the woman.

"Will you help me prepare dinner?"

Chandra was caught off guard by the query. The last time she'd offered to help Preston he'd snarled at her before relenting. "Of course I'll help you. What's on the menu?"

"I've planned to roast a rack of lamb with an herb crust, couscous, glazed carrots and homemade ice cream."

"How would you like to be my personal chef?"

"I think we can work out something?"

"How much are you going to charge me?" she asked.

"We'll begin with one kiss three times a day for the first week. Then we'll increase it to two, three times a day, for the following week."

"What happens the third week?"

"Why three, three times a week, and so on and so on."

Chandra flashed a sensual moue. "It sounds as if I'm going to have to hand out a lot of kisses."

"You can't have it both ways, beautiful. I have to charge you something."

Going on tiptoe, she wrapped her arms around Preston's neck. "Can't I at least get the family discount?"

Preston's lids came down, hiding his innermost feelings. This was the Chandra Eaton he'd come to look for: soft, sexy *and* teasing.

"You can't get a family discount until you officially become family."

Chandra knew in which direction the conversation was going, and she wanted no part of it. Fortunately, the distinctive chime from his cell phone preempted her reply.

Preston leaned in closer. "To be continued." Turning on his heels, he walked over to the cooking island to answer the phone, glancing at the name on the display. "Good morning, Ray."

"That it is, P.J.," Raymond Hardy shouted, followed by a gravelly chuckle. "Beth just gave birth to a baby girl!"

"Congratulations! How are Beth and the baby?"

"Paige is doing well, but Beth's going to be in the hospital longer than she'd expected. She had to undergo a Cesarean."

A slight frown creased Preston's forehead when Chandra opened and closed drawers in the island. He knew she was looking for pieces for place settings. She exuded a nervous energy that wouldn't permit her to sit and relax.

"It's going to be a while before she's going to feel

like doing anything around the house, I'm giving you guys a gift of a cleaning service for the next month."

There was silence before Ray spoke again. "Thanks, man. That's really going to come in handy, because my bank account is hovering around zero after I had to pay my lawyer to sue my sonofabitch ex-collaborator for selling my songs to that slimy record producer."

Preston knew Ray and his wife were strapped for cash, and paying for a cleaning service was his way of lessening their burden. He'd done the same for his sister after she delivered each of her two sets of twins. He'd also paid for a nanny with the second set, only because Yolanda was overwhelmed having to care for four young boys under the age of four.

Preston nodded although Ray couldn't see him. "There's no need to thank me. I know you can't boil water, and Beth is a little obsessive when it comes to having a clean house." The expression "One hand washes the other and both hands wash the face" came to mind. He'd asked Ray to pen the music and lyrics for *Death's Kiss,* not to offer the man a generous commission but because he was one of the best in the business.

"I'm glad you said it, because whenever I mention it she goes off on me," Ray said, laughing. "As soon as Beth is up and moving around without too much difficulty, I'll call you and we can set up another time to meet."

"Don't rush it, Ray."

"I know you, P.J. Once you get something in your head, you're like a dog with a bone. You just won't let go. Now, if you're stepping out of your comfort zone to come up with a musical drama, I know it's going to be spectacular. Tell me a little about it and I'll begin working on something on this end."

Preston gave him a brief overview of the plot. "I need music for a ball and a voodoo ritual." There was a moment of silence, and he knew Ray's mind had shifted into overdrive.

"Early nineteenth-century music and dance would include the Cotillion, English Country Dance and perhaps a Quadrille."

"Throw in a waltz and tango and you've covered all the dances."

"I can understand a waltz, because it had become quite a dance phenomena about 1790, but the tango didn't become popular outside of the ghettos of Argentina until the early twentieth century."

The reason Preston had selected Raymond Hardy to write the score was not only because the man was a musical genius but also a music history expert. He'd appeared in several documentaries chronicling the history of musical genres.

"Pascual is a vampire who originated in Argentina."

"So, he's a time-traveler," Ray said. The excitement in his voice was evident.

"You've got it," Preston confirmed.

"This is very interesting, P.J. What if I write a love theme in Spanish, French and English?"

"You're a musical genius, Ray." He hadn't told the composer about Chandra's suggestion to have a song sung in English and Spanish. Adding French would be in keeping with early nineteenth-century multicultural and multilingual New Orleans.

"You've given me a lot to work with, P.J. Let me see what I can come up with. By the way, when do you project auditioning and rehearsals?"

"Not until the spring." It would take him that long to

complete and fine-tune the dialogue. "I've decided to go local with this production. In other words, I want local raw talent. If I'm going to direct and produce, then I'll have a much smaller budget from which to work. And if Beth decides to go back to work, then I'd like her to design the sets."

"I'm sure she'll do it, even if she has to ask her mother to come up and watch Paige while she's working."

"I don't want to infringe on her time with your daughter, but she is my first choice."

"I'll ask her, and then e-mail you Beth's response. P.J.," he said after a pause, "you've got yourself another winner."

Preston stared at Chandra as she moved around the kitchen in an attempt to find what she needed to set the table in the dining area. Instead of sitting around and waiting for him to wait on her, she'd assumed a take-charge approach.

"Thanks, Ray. Give Beth my best and give Paige a kiss from her Uncle P.J."

Ray laughed again. "Will do. Later, buddy."

Preston ended the call. He'd wanted to tell Ray that he never would've come up with the premise for the play if it hadn't been for Chandra Eaton's erotic dreams and her taunt that all of his work was tragically brooding. With ethereal romantic period costumes, historically correct set decorations and star-crossed lovers, *Death's Kiss* was certain to become a stunningly visual feast, just like the sexy woman moving confidently around the kitchen.

His gaze lingered on the shapely roundness of her hips in the fitted jeans. Her conservative style of dress had artfully concealed a curvy lush body that sent his libido into overdrive.

"Thank you for setting the table. It looks very nice."

Chandra turned to face Preston. She hadn't heard him when he'd come up behind her. "You're very welcome."

"I usually don't use a tablecloth, but it does add a nice touch," he admitted.

She suspected he probably took his meals at the cooking island rather than the table, but held her tongue, because she didn't like verbally sparring with Preston. Debating an issue was one thing, but arguing over inane issues tended to upset her emotional equilibrium.

"I suppose you overheard my conversation with Ray. His wife had the baby, so it's just going to be the two of us."

"That's okay."

Preston's expressive eyebrows lifted a fraction before settling into place. "If you don't have anything on your to-do list, I'd like you to hang out here with me for a few days so we can flesh out the second act." He was anxious to finalize the plotting process so he could begin the actual writing process.

"I can't commit until tomorrow."

Belinda had promised Chandra she would let her know when a moving company would deliver the bedroom, living room and kitchen furniture, and she wanted to be available if or when a school district contacted her for an interview.

"No problem." Resting his hands on her shoulders, Preston steered Chandra to the cooking island. "I want you to sit down and relax." He settled her on a tall stool. "After breakfast we'll go on a walking tour of the valley." Resting his elbows on the granite surface, he smiled at the young woman who'd managed to fill the empty spaces in his solitary life. "Do you like blueberry buttermilk pancakes?"

Her eyes brightened like a young child's on Christmas morning. "You've got to be kidding. They're my favorite." Her eyes narrowed. "Who told you I like blueberry pancakes?"

"No one."

Chandra sat up straighter. "I don't believe you. Someone in my family *had* to tell you."

"Okay, baby, I'll tell you. It was your mother."

Heat seared her cheeks as if someone had placed a lighted match to her face. "You told my mother I was staying over with you?"

"She wanted to know if we were coming back to Paoli for brunch, so I had to tell her we were going to Kennett Square. Does my telling her upset you?"

"No."

At thirty, Chandra didn't have to rely on her parents for financial support, but she was living at home—even if it was only temporarily. If she didn't come home she didn't have to call and give an account of her whereabouts. Yet she still didn't want to advertise when she was spending the night with a man.

"I assured your mother that you were safe with me."

"Why? Because you're a nice guy?"

"Being a nice guy has nothing to do with it. It's just that I would never consciously hurt you."

The seconds ticked as Chandra's gaze met and fused with Preston's. He'd claimed he would never consciously hurt her and she suspected that neither did Laurence. But it happened. Laurence had to have known of his parents' biases, yet he'd pursued her relentlessly until she finally agreed to go out with him. Her ex-fiancé hadn't hurt her as much as he'd deceived her.

"That's nice to hear," she drawled.

"You still don't trust me, do you, Chandra?"

"I'll trust you until you give me cause not to."

Preston ran a finger down the length of her nose. "Let's hope that never happens."

Chandra flashed a smile she didn't feel. *I pray it never happens,* she mused. She knew she had to shake off the sense of distrust or she would never enjoy her relationship with Preston. Pulling back her shoulders, she exhaled a breath as her heart swelled with an emotion she'd thought she would never feel again. Despite her decision not to—she knew she was falling in love with Preston Tucker.

Chapter 12

Chandra came to a complete stop. She didn't want to believe she was that tired. Her calves were aching. After a breakfast of the most incredibly delicious pancakes she'd ever eaten, she had retreated to her bedroom where she'd put on a pair of running shoes and joined Preston as he led her on a walking tour.

The exterior of his home was as exquisite as the interior. The boxwood garden, covering a quarter acre, was a riot of exotic ferns and flowers. She'd recognized late-blooming roses, hydrangea in hues ranging from deep purple to snow white, dahlia in various colors and sizes and chrysanthemum—some that were six inches in diameter. There were sections with all white, yellow, pink and red flowers in different varieties she didn't recognize, and if she could she wouldn't be able to pronounce.

A shed several hundred feet from the rear of the

164

house was filled with cords of firewood, while two dozen stumps that would eventually become firewood were covered with a clear plastic tarp. Preston revealed he chopped wood during the winter months and worked out in his building's health club whenever he stayed over in Philadelphia to keep in shape. She'd had her answer to how he'd maintained a slender, toned physique.

Lowering her head, she rested her hands on her knees. "We're going to have to stop while I rest my legs before we start back."

Preston looped an arm around her waist. "Let's get off the road and sit down under that tree." Of the twenty miles of rolling hills and country roads that made up the Brandywine Valley, they'd covered more than five miles.

They sat down under the sweeping branches of a towering oak tree with leaves of brilliant autumnal colors in orange and yellow. The midmorning temperatures were at least ten to fifteen degrees cooler than they'd been the day before. Preston wondered whether summer was about to take its last curtain call. The next weekend would also signal the end of daylight saving time, and with it came fewer hours of daylight. He wanted to complete his first draft of *Death's Kiss* before Thanksgiving and that would give him the winter months to edit and reedit to his critical satisfaction.

Chandra, sitting between Preston's outstretched legs, rested the back of her head against his shoulder. The view from where they sat was awe-inspiring, ethereal.

"I can't believe I've lived in Pennsylvania most of my life, yet I've never visited this part of the state."

Winding several strands of Chandra's hair around his forefinger, Preston rubbed the pad of his thumb over its softness; he released it, watching as it floated into a corkscrew curl.

"You've never been to Longwood Gardens?"

She shook her head. "Unfortunately I haven't."

"Most Philadelphia schoolchildren visit the gardens at least once during a class trip."

Tilting her chin, Chandra smiled at him staring down at her. "Well, I must have had a deprived childhood."

"Where did you go to school?" Preston asked.

"My brother, sisters and I attended Chesterfield Academy."

Preston wanted to tell her that she was anything but deprived. Dr. Dwight and Roberta Eaton had enrolled their children in one of Philadelphia's most prestigious private schools, while he and his sister took advantage of the best that the public school system had to offer.

"I assume you went to Europe instead of Longwood for class trips."

Chandra placed her hands atop the larger one resting on her belly.

"Only the upperclassmen were permitted to leave the country. I spent the second half of my junior year in Spain studying and occasionally taking side trips to Portugal and France. It was the first time I was bitten by the traveling bug. I could've easily lived in a different country every year." She glanced up at Preston again. "How about you? Are you a vagabond or a homebody?"

He smiled. "I'm definitely a homebody."

"Where's your spirit of adventure?" she teased.

"My spirit of adventure means traveling first class."

Chandra shifted to face Preston, she half on, half off his body. "I think I've found my Pascual."

He frowned. "Say what?"

"You," she said. "I hadn't realized when I began developing Pascual that you and he shared similar physical and psychological characteristics. His mantra is enjoying the best immortality has to offer him."

"That's where you're wrong, Chandra. I'm not immortal."

"Okay. But do you gamble?"

"What do you mean by gamble?" he asked, answering her question with one of his own.

"Do you play cards?"

"Yes. *If* I do play, then it's either poker or blackjack."

Pressing her chest to his, Chandra brushed her mouth over his. "Perfect. Blackjack, or as the French call it, *vingt-et-un,* whist or cribbage were the popular card games during Josette's time. Poker didn't become popular until after 1830. Pascual will become quite the center of attention when he introduces a new card game known as poker."

"Poker and the tango," Preston murmured under his breath. "What other surprises does he plan to spring on the curious inhabitants of the Crescent City?"

Excitement shimmered in Chandra's eyes. "I think that's enough. The men will be caught up in the challenge of learning a new card game and the women either mesmerized or scandalized by the mysterious stranger. Can you imagine their reaction at the ball when Pascual presents himself to Josette, then leads her in a tango? It will be another one hundred years before women show their ankles, but more than an ankle will be on display that night. It will also be leg *and* thigh."

"That is scandalous," Preston concurred.

"Marie is mortified because she believes Pascual

has deliberately ruined Josette's chance to become *placée* to the man she has chosen for her. But as the night progresses, she notices many of the mothers are scheming to get Pascual to notice their daughters."

"Does he get to dance with the other young women?"

Chandra nodded. "Yes. But with them he is the perfect gentleman, mouthing the proper greetings and thanking them for permitting him to bask in their beauty. One minute he's there, then as a rush of air comes into the ballroom, causing candles to flicker, he's gone."

Preston went completely still. He could see the scene being played out in his head. Chandra had just given him what he needed to set the stage for the all-important, very dramatic act two.

"When does Josette see him again?"

"He's waiting in her bedroom when she returns from the ball. He hides behind a dressing screen while her maid enters the room to help her ready herself for bed. But Josette orders her out, saying she doesn't need her assistance. After the woman leaves, Josette locks the door and closes the casement windows.

"Pascual emerges from behind the screen. He steps into the role as maid and seducer when he removes the pins from Josette's hair, then removes her dress. This scene must be very sensual, Preston. The actors aren't going to have sex onstage. However, they must give the illusion that they are making love. Perhaps this scene can take place where the audience views it through a sheer curtain as if peering through a bedroom window with a single candle for illumination. The lighting will become as much a character as Josette and Pascual.

"When the scene ends, there shouldn't be a sound in the theater. It will be your test as the director that your actors have hypnotized the audience. Every woman should want to be on the stage and in that bed with Pascual, and the same with every man, who is telling himself that he is *the one* seducing the beautiful young virgin. Once the lighting fades to black and there is stunned silence you'll know immediately that you've hit the mark."

Preston was hard-pressed not to make love to Chandra. The scene she'd just described was exactly as she had written in her journal. She'd prepared herself for bed and instead of a lamp, she'd lit a candle. The candle was about to burn out when her mysterious lover enters the room. Chandra had described the lovemaking scene so vividly that Preston felt not like a voyeur but a participant in the act.

"That's not going to be an easy feat, because I've never directed a love scene."

Chandra placed her fingertips over his mouth. "It's not about the dialogue, darling. It's all about what is visual, and therefore sensual. If I were sitting in the audience I would want to hear the sound of her hairpins when they fall to the floor and the whisper of fabric being removed as they undress."

Capturing her wrist, Preston pulled the delicate hand away from his mouth. "Do you want to hear them make love?"

Chandra's brow flickered with indecision. "No," she said after a lengthy pause. "I think it would cheapen the scene. It's not a porno flick, where the sounds are essential to the movie. I believe it would work better if Josette would gasp aloud when Pascual penetrates her. This will let the audience know that she is indeed a virgin. It could conclude with a sigh of satisfaction—

again making the audience aware that the lovemaking was wonderful."

"You've missed your calling, Chandra."

She shook her head. "I've never wanted to act."

"I'm not talking about acting."

"What are you talking about?"

Bringing her hand to his mouth, Preston pressed a kiss to the palm. "Writing."

"Thanks for the compliment, but I've never been interested in writing. I prefer to read."

Preston's gaze narrowed when he saw dark clouds moving in from the west. He stood up, bringing Chandra up with him. "I think we better head back because it looks as if we're in for some rain." He pointed. "Look at those clouds."

Chandra didn't need a second warning when she saw how dark the sky had become. She forgot about the pain in her legs when she jogged alongside Preston when they headed in the direction of the house. She'd been so engrossed in talking about *Death's Kiss* that she hadn't noticed the weather had changed.

The wind had picked up, gusts swirling leaves and twigs. Rain had begun falling when the house came into view, then came down in torrents by the time they reached the back door. The wet clothes pasted to Chandra's body raised goose bumps; her teeth were chattering when Preston unlocked the door and deactivated the security system.

"I'm going to take a shower," she announced as she kicked off her soggy running shoes.

Preston, following suit, slipped out of his running shoes. He stripped off his shirt, jeans and underwear, dropping them in a large wicker basket in the space that doubled as a laundry and mudroom.

Walking on bare feet, he made his way into the half bath off the kitchen. Stepping in the shower stall, he turned on the water, gritting his teeth as icy pellets fell on his head. Then he adjusted the temperature to lukewarm. Preston lingered long enough to shampoo his cropped hair and wash his body.

His mind was a maelstrom of vivid images of what Chandra had suggested for the play's second act as he stepped out and dried himself with a bath sheet. He hadn't lied when he told her she should've been a writer. She was an untapped talent, her fertile mind lying fallow; all that was needed was a kernel of an idea to yield a harvest worthy of a literary feast.

He was Preston J. Tucker, the critically acclaimed dramatist who'd won awards, was the recipient of a McArthur genius grant and who had been compared to some of the most celebrated playwrights of the past century. However, when he compared what he'd written and produced to what he was currently collaborating on with Chandra, it paled in comparison.

Chandra had what he lacked: a highly developed sense of visualization. He relied on strong dialogue, characterization and simplistic costuming and stark sets to tell his message, while Chandra added the element of sensual visuals.

The big screen would be the perfect vehicle for *Death's Kiss*. Love scenes could be performed without the limitations that usually went along with a stage production. Nudity on the stage wasn't taboo, but Preston found it more a hindrance than an enticement to put theatergoers in seats. Once the initial shock of frontal nudity was assuaged—then what? He'd always asked himself whether the production would've stood on its own merits without the nudity. If the answer was yes, then he deleted it.

Wrapping the terry cloth fabric around his waist, he walked out of the bath, heading toward his bedroom. The connecting door was ajar and he could hear Chandra opening and closing drawers. Preston would've suggested they share a shower, but he didn't want a repeat of what had happened earlier that morning.

It took Herculean strength for him to pull out when he realized he was making love to Chandra without a condom. He'd pulled out when it had been the last thing he'd wanted to do, and he knew then he wasn't the same person he'd been before meeting her.

Preston believed that he would eventually marry and father children, but *when* was the question. He'd celebrated his thirty-eighth birthday March seventeenth, and as he'd done since turning thirty-five, he went through a period of self-examination, asking himself if he was satisfied with what he'd accomplished, had he learned not to repeat past mistakes, did he like who he was and what he'd become and finally if he was ready to share himself and what he'd accomplished with someone with whom he would spend the rest of his life. All the questions yielded an affirmative. The exception was the last one.

His passion for writing had become paramount, and jealously guarded his privacy and his time. But that had changed with Chandra Eaton. It was as if he couldn't get enough of her—in and out of bed. She hadn't shocked him when she had taken him into her mouth. It was more of a surprise because he hadn't expected it. He'd suspected she was capable of great passion because of what she'd written in her journal, but he still hadn't known whether her dreams were real or imagined. That no longer mattered because he wanted Chandra Eaton to be the last woman in his life.

Dropping the towel on the padded bench at the foot of the bed, he'd pulled on a pair of boxer-briefs, sweatpants and a long-sleeved tee when he heard a groan. Taking long strides, he crossed the room, opened the door wider to find Chandra writhing on the bed, clutching the back of her leg. She had on a bra and a pair of bikini panties.

His heartbeat kicked into a higher rhythm as he sat on the side of the bed. Reaching for her, he pressed her face to his chest. "What's the matter, baby?"

"My leg," she gasped as the muscle tightened even more.

"Move your hand."

Preston stared at the lump that had come up on the back of her calf. "It looks as if you have a muscle cramp. I'm going to have to massage it to get the blood flowing again."

He'd experienced enough cramps when he'd played football in high school, and then in college, to last him several lifetimes. His interest in competitive sports ended once he broke his nose. After it healed a plastic surgeon wanted to reset it, but he didn't want to have to relive the pain that left his face bruised and swollen for weeks.

Chandra had experienced severe menstrual cramps, but the pain in her leg surpassed any she'd had. "Please don't massage it too hard," she said between clenched teeth.

Preston's fingers grazed the tight area. "I'm going to cover your calf with a warm cloth before I massage it."

She half rose from the bed. "Aren't you supposed to ice it?"

"I'll ice it later."

He entered the bathroom, wet a facecloth under running hot water and returned to the bedroom to place it over Chandra's leg. Lying beside her, he kissed the end of her nose. "Did it just cramp up?"

Chandra's smile came out like a grimace. "It was bothering me earlier."

"Why didn't you say something?"

"I'd asked you to stop so I could rest my legs."

"Resting your legs isn't the same as saying you had a leg cramp."

She closed her eyes, shutting out his thunderous expression. "There's no need to get testy, Preston. It's not that critical."

"That's your opinion."

Chandra opened her eyes and glared at him glaring back at her. "If you're spoiling for a fight, then you won't get one from me, Preston Tucker, because with the pain that's kicking my butt I might say something that wouldn't be very intelligent or ladylike."

Preston counted slowly to three. He wasn't about to get into it with Chandra over something that didn't warrant an argument. If she'd told him that her leg was hurting, then he would've suggested they put off walking for another time.

"I don't fight with women."

"My bad," she drawled. "I meant argue."

"And I don't argue with women."

Another spasm gripped Chandra, preempting her comeback. "Argh-h!"

Galvanized into action, Preston moved to the foot of the bed. Removing the cloth, he kneaded the area gently with his thumbs, alternating applying pressure with massaging her calf. Fifteen minutes into his ministration, the lump disappeared.

"Don't move," Preston said in a soft voice. "I'm going to get some ice."

Chandra couldn't move when she felt him get up off the bed, even if her life depended upon it. She'd endured the most excruciating pain possible, and now that it was gone she feared moving because she didn't know if it would return.

She gasped again, this time when icy cold penetrated her limb. Preston had filled a plastic bag with ice, pressed it against her calf and covered it with a towel to absorb the moisture.

She gave him a dazzling smile when he lay beside her again. "I'm sorry I snapped at you." He stared at her under heavy lids, and she thought he wasn't going to accept her apology.

"Are you really sorry, or are you saying it because you think that's what I want to hear?"

Unbidden tears filled her eyes, shocking Chandra. She was the Eaton girl who rarely cried. Even when she fell and hurt herself she refused to cry. She was the tough tomboy sister who threw tantrums when she had to wear a dress, while Donna and Belinda loved playing dress-up with frilly dresses and high heels.

The first and only time she'd become hysterical was when she'd returned to the States for a family emergency and was told that her sister and brother-in-law had been killed by a drunk driver. Her father had contacted her in Belize, but refused to tell her what the emergency was until she walked through the front door of her parents' house to find everyone waiting for her—everyone but Donna.

Preston froze when he saw the tears well up in Chandra's eyes. Lines of concern etched his forehead. "What's the matter, baby?"

She sniffed back the tears before they fell. "I don't know. I suppose falling in love..." Her words trailed off when she realized what she was about to admit.

Preston's eyes narrowed. "What did you say?"

"Forget it."

"I don't think so, Chandra Eaton. Either you finish what you were going to say or I'm going to hold you hostage until you do."

"That's kidnapping."

His frown deepened. "Am I supposed to be scared?"

"No. I'm just warning you that kidnapping is a crime."

Threading his fingers through her hair, Preston cupped the back of her head in his hand. "It can't be a crime if you willingly come with me. Even your mother knows that." His fingers tightened on her scalp. "Now, who are you in love with?"

Chandra felt as if her brain was in tumult. Her feelings for Preston intensified each time she saw him, which led to ambivalence and confusion. She'd always thought of herself as levelheaded, independent and able to survive without having a man in her life.

She found Preston different from the other men in her life because he was a man in every sense of the word while the others were boys masquerading as men. He was straightforward and not into mind games.

Once she realized who he was, she'd thought his ego would surpass his talent, but it was just the opposite. When she'd introduced him to her family he appeared uncomfortable with his celebrity status.

Preston stared at her without blinking. "I need to know if there's someone else so I can walk away before I find myself in too deep."

Panic shot through Chandra like a volt of electricity. Preston was talking about walking away when that was the last thing she wanted him to do. She'd admitted to Denise that if love did come knocking, then she was going to hold on to it as if her life was at stake.

"There's no one else." She rolled her eyes upward in supplication. "I swore a vow that I would never fall in love again but…" She pounded his shoulder with her fist.

Mindful of her leg, Preston gathered Chandra until she lay atop him. "It serves you right for making promises you can't keep. I've never said I wouldn't fall in love, so I'm not as conflicted as you."

Her head came up and she met his amused stare. "What are you talking about?"

"I have no problem admitting that I love you."

Chandra froze. "You love me?" The three words were pregnant with uncertainty.

"Yes. Why do you look so startled?"

"I thought we were just friends."

"Yeah, right," he drawled. "You're delusional, baby, if you believe that."

Her smile was dazzling. "How about friends with benefits?"

Preston winked at her. "There you go."

They lay together, each lost in their private thoughts. Chandra couldn't believe she'd confessed to a man she'd known a mere two weeks that she was in love with him.

Each time she left home her parents claimed she'd changed. She may have looked different outwardly, but inwardly she hadn't changed that much. It took living in Belize for more than two years as a volunteer teacher to change her completely.

She'd left the States a girl and returned a woman.

The dark sky and the rhythmic tapping of rain against the windows lulled both of them into a protective cocoon where any and everything ceased to exist outside their cloistered world reserved for lovers.

Chapter 13

Chandra felt as if she was on the merry-go-round of eternal bliss and that she never wanted to get off.

She'd returned from the Brandywine Valley filled with a joy that prompted her to pinch herself to make certain she wasn't dreaming. She and Preston had stayed over until Monday afternoon, because she had to clean her apartment. The delivery of furniture that had been in Belinda's house was scheduled for Thursday. Preston had offered his cleaning service, but she'd turned him down because she needed to work off the tension that usually accompanied the onset of her menses.

The shipping company contacted her with the news that her trunk had arrived from Belize and wanted to set up a time for a delivery. She gave them her new address, and the trunk arrived an hour after all the other furniture was set up in the one-bedroom co-op with views of the riverside park dubbed Penn's Landing.

She'd just emptied the steamer trunk and covered it with a colorful handwoven Indian rug in the space near the door when the intercom rang, startling her.

Pressing a button, she spoke softly into the speaker. "Yes."

"I have a delivery for Ms. C. Eaton," announced a slightly accented male voice.

"Come on up." She pressed another button, disengaging the lock on the outer door.

Once the furniture was set up in its respective rooms, Chandra realized the space was much larger than she'd originally thought. Denise had had the walls painted a soft oyster-white and the wood floors sanded and covered with polyurethane, so all she had to do was wipe away layers of dust and clean the kitchen, bathroom and refrigerator. Her apartment was one of four on the top floor of a six-story building, which meant she didn't have to deal with someone making noise over her head.

The doorbell chimed Beethoven's Ninth Symphony. Denise had installed a programmable doorbell. Chandra had gone through the selections, deciding on a sample of the classical masterpiece.

She peered through the security eye. "Who is it?"

"Pascual."

Chandra opened the door to find Preston holding a vase filled with a large bouquet of pink and white roses and a bottle of champagne. "You are so crazy." She opened the door wider. "Please come in."

Dipping his head, Preston gave her a searing kiss. "Congratulations. Your place is beautiful." He handed her the bottle of champagne. "Should I take off my shoes?" The light coming from an overhead Tiffany-style hanging fixture reflected off the floor.

She smiled at him. Tonight he wore a pair of gray

flannel slacks, navy blue mohair jacket, stark white shirt and purple silk tie. "No."

Preston debated, then slipped out of his slip-ons, walking in sock-covered feet and following Chandra into a living room with a white seating group with differing blue accessories.

"You can put the vase on the dining area table." Chandra indicated a solid oak oval pedestal table with seating for six. She climbed four steps to the kitchen and opened the refrigerator, placing the champagne on a shelf.

She'd gone to the supermarket the day before to fill the pantry with staples and the refrigerator with perishables. She didn't have a car, so she willingly paid to have her order delivered. Chandra wasn't certain how she would be able to get around without a car despite living in the city and having access to public transportation. Turning, she held out her arms and wasn't disappointed when Preston moved into her embrace. It'd been five days since she last saw him, but it could've been fifty-five.

"I have an interview for a position as a fifth-grade social studies teacher."

She'd checked her e-mail and received responses from two school districts. One wanted her to fill in for a special education teacher on leave, despite her not having special education certification, and the other, within walking distance, had advertised for a permanent substitute position. She'd called, setting up an appointment as a substitute.

Picking her up, Preston swung her around. "Congratulations!"

Tightening her hold on his neck, Chandra stared at the man to whom she'd given her love and her heart. How had she forgotten the sensual curve of his sexy mouth, the little tuft of hair under his lip and the hooded, brilliantly intelligent dark eyes. Then there was the body—the lean, muscled physique under tailored attire that made her crave him whether they were together or apart.

"Congratulate me *after* I get the position."

He smiled, the gesture tilting the corners of his mobile mouth upward. "I know you'll get it."

"Because you say so?"

Preston's gaze dropped to her mouth. "Because I know so."

"You're biased, Preston."

"I am when it concerns you."

"Put me down, Preston."

"Why?"

"Because I want to show you the rest of the apartment."

"You can show me the rest of the apartment after we get back."

"Where are we going, Preston?"

"We are going out to dinner."

Chandra stared at Preston as if he'd lost his mind. "I can't go out. Look at my hair. Look at me." She'd made an appointment for a full beauty makeover the day before her interview.

"I am looking at you, and you're beautiful. Remember when I wanted to take you to Le Bec-Fin and we had to postpone until another time?" Chandra nodded. "I tried to get a reservation for tonight, but they were booked. So, I decided to surprise the love of my life and take her to the Moshulu instead."

A smile spread across Chandra like the rays of the rising sun. "Put me down so I can change out of these jeans and into something a little less casual."

182 *Sweet Dreams*

Preston kissed Chandra with his eyes before his mouth covered hers in a hot, hungry kiss. "Don't take too long." He lowered her until her feet touched the floor. "Go, before I change my mind and—"

"And what, Preston?"

"And have you for an appetizer, salad, entrée and dessert."

Taking a step, Chandra pressed her breasts to his hard chest. "Start counting. I'll be ready within fifteen minutes."

Preston sat across the table from Chandra in the main dining room on the permanently docked tall ship overlooking the Delaware River. If it had been warmer or earlier in the year, he would've reserved one of the open-air upper decks. He couldn't pull his gaze away from her face.

They'd ordered chilled jumbo shrimp with a horse-radish cocktail sauce from the raw bar and an appetizer of crispy duck wontons filled with hoisin barbecue duck confit and scallions and covered with a sweet soy glaze and chopped cilantro. Both passed on the soup and salad. Chandra's entrée choice was Gulf Coast mahimahi, while Preston selected the Amish chicken breast.

It'd taken her exactly fifteen minutes to change from a pullover and jeans and into a black wool sheath dress ending at her knees, matching sheer hose and suede pumps. A mauve hip-length mohair jacket pulled her winning look together. His gaze caressed her lightly made-up face—a face displayed to its best advantage with her shoulder-length hair fashioned into a classic chignon.

"You look incredibly beautiful tonight," he whispered reverently. "And if you tell me I'm biased I'm going to kiss you until you lose your breath," Preston threatened.

Chandra took a breath and affected a demure smile. Not seeing Preston for several days had afforded her time to step back and assess their whirlwind relationship. At first she'd begun second-guessing herself, believing it was because of her collaborating with him on *Death's Kiss* that Preston felt the need to profess to love her. That it all would come to a screeching halt once he completed the play.

Then she woke one morning, shaking with fear and uncertainty from a disturbing dream. It was upsetting because it was the first dream she'd had since returning from Belize. Unlike the others, in this one she could see a man's face. He was laughing and pointing at her, while others joined in with their own derisive mockery. She hadn't wanted to believe it, but the man was Preston Tucker.

She'd reached for her cell with the intent of calling and telling him she couldn't continue to see him, but her fingers refused to follow the dictates of her brain. Once she recovered from the terrifying nightmare, Chandra knew her distrust of men had reared its ugly head.

However, what she felt for Preston was real, pure. She hadn't fallen in love with Preston J. Tucker, award-winning playwright. She'd fallen in love with Preston, the man.

She loved him, Denise was in awe of him, Griffin had taken on the responsibility of representing him professionally and her parents liked him. Whenever she spoke to Roberta, she always asked about Preston.

"Thank you, Preston."

Chandra wanted to tell Preston he looked deliciously handsome, but couldn't get her tongue to form the words. *What the hell is wrong with me?* She managed to get one of Philly's most eligible bachelors to date her exclusively; meanwhile she was acting like an uptight snob who seemed not to want to give him the time of day.

Reaching across the table, Preston took Chandra's hand. He smiled, but the warm gesture did not reach his eyes. They were cold, his expression a mask of stone. "What's the matter?" he asked perceptively.

"Nothing, darling."

"Don't darling me, Chandra. I know when something is bothering you."

"Have you suddenly become clairvoyant, or have you always been able to read minds?"

Preston decided to ignore her acerbic retort. Something *was* bothering her and he intended to uncover what it was. Perhaps something or someone was bothering her. When he spoke to Chandra on Tuesday, she'd mentioned she had menstrual cramps, and that meant he had to wait to make love to her.

"No, but I grew up in a house with two females, so I'm familiar with them PMSing."

Chandra rolled her eyes. "For your information, I'm finished with my cycle," she whispered.

"If it's not that, then what is it, Chandra?"

She knew she had to tell Preston what had her on edge. "I had a dream the other night."

Preston's impassive expression did not change with her revelation. He'd waited weeks for her to tell him about the dreams that had become the foundation for his latest work. "Do you want to tell me about it?"

Chandra told him—everything. She saw his gaze grow hard, resentful. If they hadn't been in a public place, she knew she wouldn't have been able to rein in her emotions.

Preston signaled for the waiter, then reached into the pocket of his slacks to leave two large bills on the table. Pushing back his chair, he stood, came around the table and helped Chandra to her feet. He'd heard enough.

"Let's get out of here."

Chandra quickened her pace to keep up with Preston's longer legs. "Will you please slow down." She was half jogging and half running, and in a pair of heels. "What's going on, Preston?"

Tightening his grip on her hand, Preston shortened his stride. He had to leave the restaurant, or else cause a scene and bring attention to himself and Chandra. He'd grown up listening to his parents bicker and snipe at each other, and that was something he wanted to avoid, at all costs, with Chandra.

They were steps from her building when he felt composed enough to explain why he'd left the restaurant so abruptly. "When are you going to learn to trust me, Chandra? I'm aware that we've only been together a month, and I don't believe I've ever given you cause to mistrust me. I haven't dated or looked at another woman since we've been together. What is it you want? Tell me, what do I have to do?"

Chandra moved closer to Preston as much to feed off his body's heat as for solace. "I never said you cheated on me."

"You didn't have to," he countered. "What you refuse to do is trust me to love you, protect you, or to be there for you."

"You're overreacting."

"Hell, yeah, I'm overreacting. You can't tell me you weren't bothered by your dream if you keep looking at me sideways and hoping I'll mess up so you'll have an excuse to send me packing."

"That's not true, Preston."

"It has to be true, Chandra."

"Are you calling me a liar, Preston?"

"All I'm saying is that I don't believe you."

Chandra stopped abruptly, causing Preston to lose his footing. However, he recovered quickly, glaring down at her like an avenging angel. The streetlamps threw long and short shadows over his face, distorting his pleasant features.

She threw up her free hand. "I don't know what I can do or say to convince you that I *do* trust you."

Preston's eyes narrowed. "There is one thing you can do."

Pulling back her shoulders, she raised her chin. "What?"

A beat passed. "Marry me."

There came another pause before Chandra asked, "You're kidding, aren't you?"

"Do I look like I'm kidding?" Preston retorted.

Chandra started to walk, but she was thwarted when Preston pulled her back to where he stood. Her temper flared, invisible tongues of red-hot fire sweeping up her chest, scorching her face. "Do not play with me." She'd enunciated each word as if he were hard of hearing.

"I'm too old to play games, Chandra. I'm going to ask you one more time if you want to marry me, and if I don't get an answer, then I'm going to walk away and never look back."

Chandra swallowed in an attempt to relieve the constriction in her throat. Preston Tucker was asking what every normal woman wanted the man with whom they'd fallen in love to ask: *Will you marry me?*

Meanwhile, she stood like a statue on the spot, her tongue frozen between her palate and her teeth. All the while her heart was beating so fast she was certain she was going to faint.

Somewhere between sanity and insanity, good and evil, right and wrong she found a modicum of strength. Preston was right—they'd only known each other a month—four short, intense, passionate weeks in which she was able to communicate—in and out of bed—with a man who treated her as his equal. She didn't know whether it was fate, serendipity or destiny that she'd left her case in that taxi for Preston Tucker to find, but Chandra knew she had to believe something beyond her control deemed that Preston would become a part of her life and her future.

She panicked, a riot of emotions attacking her from all sides when he released her hand.

He was going to walk!

She couldn't let him walk!

"Yes!" The single word was a shriek. "Yes, Preston, I will marry you." She was shaking, tears were flowing, and Chandra wasn't certain how much longer her quivering legs would be able to aid her in remaining upright.

Preston felt his knees buckle slightly before he drew himself up to his full height. He'd gambled *and* he'd won. He hadn't seen Chandra in five days, but it'd taken only one for him to realize why he'd been drawn to her and why he wanted her not only in his life but also a part of his life.

He'd dated women much more beautiful, women who could buy and sell a man with the scrawl of a signature on a bank check and women so eager to please that they'd sell themselves for any price. Women whose names and faces paled in comparison to the one standing before him.

Preston knew Chandra was the *one* within seconds of the elevator doors opening, and he'd come face-to-face with the woman who'd recorded her erotic dreams.

Cradling her face between his hands, he kissed her quivering mouth, then her tears. "Shush-h-h. Don't cry, baby. We're going to have a wonderful life together."

Preston's attempt to console Chandra elicited more tears. Moving closer, she cupped his hands. "I love you so much," she whispered against his parted lips.

"Come home with me, baby." He'd punctuated each word with a kiss at each corner of her mouth.

"Why?"

"I want to make love to you."

Chandra smiled through the moisture shimmering on her lashes like minute raindrops. "We don't have to go to your place. I have protection. And I'll treat you to breakfast in bed if you decide to spend the night."

Preston kissed the end of her nose. "You are incredible."

"Thank you." She wanted to tell the man she'd promised to marry that *he* was incredible, because he'd gotten her to fall in love and agree to marry him within the span of a month.

"We can't sleep in too late tomorrow because I want to take you shopping for an engagement ring."

Chandra nodded numbly. The enormity of what she'd agreed had become apparent with the mention of a ring. She'd taken a step forward, and now it was too late to backtrack.

"I think there's something very wrong with us, Preston, if we always end up sucking face in public."

Preston smiled. "On that note, we should head upstairs."

Chandra and Preston shared a secret smile as they rode the elevator to the sixth floor. No words were needed. Everything they wanted to say had been said.

After closing and locking the door, Chandra reached for her fiancé's hand, leading him in the direction of her bedroom. She hadn't drawn the silk drapes and sheers at the wall-to-wall windows and the light from a full moon silvered every light-colored object in the room. She took her time undressing Preston: shoes, socks, jacket, tie, cuff links, shirt, belt, slacks and briefs. Smiling, she presented him with her back.

Fastening his mouth to the column of Chandra's scented neck, Preston nipped the delicate skin. He'd become Pascual and Chandra, Josette, he undressing Josette with the intent of claiming her innocence. But instead of a flowing gown with an Empire waistline it was a circa twenty-first-century jacket, dress, stockings and shoes. He searched for the pins in her hair, letting them fall, one by one onto the floor, the sound reverberating in the stillness of the space.

The sound of Chandra's breathing quickened when he removed her bra, followed by her bikini panties. "I love you so much," Preston whispered reverently, pressing his mouth and body to her soft, scented flesh.

Splaying his hands over her back, fingertips tracing, sculpting her ribs, the indentation of her waist and her rounded hips. He pulled her closer to feel the heaviness of his sex stirring between his thighs.

Throwing back her head, Chandra gasped when his rising hardness moved against her mound. Going on tiptoe, she looped her arms around Preston's neck in an attempt to get closer. She was on fire and needed him to extinguish the blaze that threatened to incinerate her.

A shudder ripped through her, bathing the area at the apex of her thighs with a rush of moisture. "Please!"

Preston heard Chandra's desperate cry, echoing his own need to bury his flesh inside her. Bending slightly, he swept her up and carried her to the bed. Supporting his body on his hands, he smiled at the dreamy expression on her face. It was his turn to gasp with the back flow of blood to his penis.

Breathing heavily, he lowered his head and tried to think of anything but the woman under him. "Give… me…the condom, baby," he stammered.

Chandra's response was to grasp his sex and ease it into her moist warmth. She gasped again. The impact of having Preston inside her without the barrier of latex was shockingly pleasurable. Raising her hips, she wound her legs around his waist, allowing for deeper penetration.

Preston rode Chandra like a man possessed, then without warning he reversed their positions. He cupped her breasts, squeezing them gently as an expression of carnality swept over her features.

He'd always liked assuming the more dominant missionary-style position, but having Chandra on top, she setting the rhythm, made it easier to prolong ejaculating.

Chandra stared at her lover as she raised her hips and grasped his testicles, squeezing them gently as he had her breasts. A grin split her face when he groaned and bucked like a wild stallion.

Holding the sac cradling his seed, she slid up and down the length of his sex, quickening and slowing and setting a cadence that kept him completely off balance.

She felt the contractions as the walls of her vagina convulsed, then Chandra didn't remember much after that as she surrendered to the orgasms overlapping one another in their intensity to take her beyond herself.

Preston captured Chandra's mouth as she exhaled the last of her passion. Tucking her curves into his, he reversed their position, his hips pumping as he released his passion inside her wet heat.

They lay together, bodies joined and moist from their lovemaking while waiting for their respiration to resume a normal pace. Supporting his greater weight on his elbows, Preston trailed light kisses over her forehead, cheek and ear.

"I never would've imagined you could feel so good," he murmured in her ear.

"Nor I you," Chandra whispered.

"We better think about setting a date, because I don't want you walking down the aisle sporting a baby bump."

Chandra opened her eyes, trying to make out Preston's expression in the muted light. "That's not going to happen."

"What's not going to happen?"

"I can't get pregnant because I have protection." She explained that she'd been fitted with an intrauterine device that could be easily removed whenever she decided that she wanted to become pregnant. "It can be left in up to five years."

Preston froze. "You want to wait five years before we have a baby?"

"Of course not, Preston. In five years I'll be in the high-risk category."

"And I'll be old as dirt. I don't want white hair by the time my son or daughter goes to school for the first time. The first time some kid asks mine if I'm his or her grandfather I'm going to lose it."

"Don't worry, sweetheart. I don't intend to wait that long."

"When do you want to get married?" he asked.

"How about June?"

Preston smiled. "June sounds good. How long do you want to wait before we start trying for a baby?"

Chandra loved children but she'd found it hard to imagine herself a mother. This was something she'd verbalized to Laurence after he'd proposed. His response was he would leave that decision to her. If she wanted a baby it was okay with him, and if she didn't then he was content not to become a father. His rationale left her unsettled because she'd suspected he didn't want children. But, on the other hand, Preston had let it be known that he wanted a family.

"We can start on our honeymoon."

Preston felt his chest fill with an emotion that nearly overwhelmed him as he tried imagining the joy of becoming a father. "Thank you."

Chapter 14

Chandra and Preston spent more than two hours at Safian & Rudolph Jewelers on Seventh and Sansom Street Sunday afternoon. It took over an hour for her to select a setting, then she had to decide on the cut and clarity of the center stone. She'd watched in amazement as the jeweler set a near-flawless two-carat cushion-cut diamond into prongs that were surrounded by pavé diamonds. The center diamond, pavé and sixty round diamonds on, along and under the platinum band totaled three point twenty carats. Seeing the ring on her left hand made it all real. She was officially engaged to marry Preston Japheth Tucker.

She sat beside Preston in his SUV, her heart beating rapidly when they shared a smile. The light coming through the windshield reflected off the brilliance of the stones on her left hand.

"We're going to have to tell our families."

Preston ran a hand over her hair. "I'll call my mother and sister later. You're going to have to let me know when you can go to Charleston so you can meet my family."

"I can go during the winter recess."

Leaning to his right, Preston kissed her. "I'll call Yolanda and tell her to expect us."

"Do you always stay with your sister?"

"Yes. But only because she's a stay-at-home mom."

"Speaking of mothers. I'm going to call mine to see if she's home so we can give her the good news."

Preston waited in the parking lot while Chandra called her mother. The call lasted less than a minute. The Eatons were home. Shifting into Reverse, he maneuvered out of the lot and into traffic. He found it ironic that he and Chandra had had prior engagements but hadn't married their respective fiancée and fiancé for all right reasons.

"Mama didn't tell me Belinda and Griffin were coming over," Chandra said when Preston maneuvered into the driveway and came to a stop behind the hybrid SUV.

Preston cut off the engine and unbuckled his seat belt. "I spoke to Griffin the other night and he told me to ask you when it will be a good time to get together."

"How about next weekend?"

"Friday or Saturday?" he asked. Preston needed to know, because he wanted to take Chandra and her sister and brother-in-law out to dinner.

"Friday."

Resting his arm along the back of her seat, he angled his head. "What if we ask them to stay over?"

"I'll ask Belinda. And before you ask, I think

spending the night in Kennett Square is preferable to the city."

Preston gave her a wink. "I was hoping you'd say that."

Chandra waited for Preston to get out and come around the vehicle to assist her. The front door opened before she rang the doorbell.

Roberta, wearing her perennial apron when at home, smiled at her daughter and the man who no doubt had settled her down. "Please come in. We were just sitting down to eat."

Chandra kissed her mother's cheek. "We didn't come to eat, Mama."

"Why did you come?"

She extended her left hand. "To show you this?"

Roberta pressed a hand to her ample bosom. "Oh, my word! You're engaged. Dwight, come here! Your baby is getting married." Chandra walked around her mother when Roberta began tugging on Preston's arm.

"What is Bertie yelling about?" Dwight Eaton asked Chandra when she met him in the middle of the living room.

"You'll have to ask her, Daddy." She would let her mother break the news of her engagement. "Where's Belinda?"

Dwight gestured over his shoulder. "She is in the kitchen. Griffin and the girls are in the family room watching television."

Chandra kissed her father before she walked into the kitchen. Belinda stood at the stove stirring a pot. The high school history teacher wore a peach-colored cashmere twinset, black wool slacks and matching patent leather slip-ons. Although she'd admitted to being pregnant, her body had not yet begun to show signs that she was carrying a child.

"Hey, sistah!"

Belinda put down the wooden spoon, replacing the cover on a pot of mustard greens. "Hey, yourself. I didn't expect to see you today."

"How are you feeling?" Chandra whispered.

Belinda hugged her sister. "Aside from hurling every morning, I'm good."

"Have you told Mama?"

"Not yet. I told Griffin that I'm tired of hiding and that I'm going to make the announcement today."

Chandra tucked her left hand behind her thigh. "I suppose that'll make two of us making announcements today."

"You're pregnant?" Belinda asked, whispering.

Chandra rolled her eyes, while sucking her teeth. "No!" She extended her hand. "But I am engaged."

Belinda closed her eyes, covered her mouth before screaming into her cupped hands. "Oh, my heavens! I can't believe my sister is going to marry Preston Tucker." She lowered her hands and reached for Chandra's. "Congratulations. Your ring is gorgeous." She glanced around. "Where's your fiancé?"

"Daddy's probably giving him the third degree."

"I suppose he doesn't want a repeat of what happened between you and Laurence Breslin."

"Trust me, Belinda, there is no comparison."

"I hear you," Belinda crooned, raising her hand for a high five handshake.

Preston walked into the kitchen with his future mother- and father-in-law to find Chandra and Belinda laughing and hugging like teenagers.

"What's all the noise about?" Everyone turned to find

Griffin, Layla and Sabrina crowding under the entrance to the kitchen.

Belinda winked at her husband. "Chandra and Preston have some good news."

"They're having a baby, too," Griffin blurted out, then clapped a hand over his mouth.

"What do you mean, 'too'?" Dwight and Roberta chorused.

Layla ducked under Griffin's arm. "Who's having a baby, Uncle Griff?"

"Yes, Griffin," Roberta drawled, "who's having a baby?"

"Belinda and I are having a baby," he announced proudly.

Roberta put up a hand, mumbling a prayer of thanks. "I had to wait twelve years for another grandchild, then we get Adam, and now we can look forward to another one next year. The Lord surely is good."

Sabrina pushed her way into the middle of the kitchen. "Layla and I are going to have a sister or brother, or will it be a cousin?"

Griffin hugged his nieces. "He or she will be whatever you want them to be."

Layla smiled, showing off the colorful bands on her clear braces. "When will we see our sister or brother?"

Belinda's gaze swept over those standing in the kitchen. "May. By the way, I'm not the only one with good news today." Her eyebrows lifted when she looked at Chandra and then Preston. "Sis?"

Chandra took three steps, reaching for Preston's hand. "Preston proposed and I accepted. We plan to marry next June."

Griffin slapped Preston on the back. "Welcome to the family, buddy."

Layla sidled up to Chandra. "Can Brina and I be bridesmaids?"

Chandra kissed her niece. "Of course you can. Lindy, I know we're going to cut it close, but I'd like for you to be my matron of honor."

Crossing her arms over her chest, Belinda gave her sister a long, penetrating look. "That may pose a problem. I'm due to deliver at the end of May, and even if you marry at the end of June, that's not enough time for me to recuperate. And even if I did feel well enough to put up with fittings and rehearsals, I plan to breast-feed."

Chandra bit her lower lip. "I'd planned to ask Denise to be in the wedding party. I suppose she'll have to be my maid of honor."

"We could always change the date." Everyone turned to look at Preston.

Chandra stared at her fiancé as if he'd taken leave of his senses. "Change it to when, Preston?"

"Thanksgiving, Christmas or even New Year's."

"You're kidding?"

"Do I look like I'm kidding?" Preston said, repeating what he'd said the night before.

Roberta stared at her husband, and he nodded. "Everyone, let's go in the family room. Chandra and Preston need to discuss something."

Sabrina balked. "I want to know when the wedding is."

Griffin put an arm around his nieces, leading them out of the kitchen. "Your aunt and her fiancé have to—"

"Discuss grown-folk business," the twins chorused,

completing the statement they'd heard countless times.

"How did my favorite girls get so smart?" Griffin teased.

Waiting until they were alone, Chandra gave Preston her undivided attention. "Do you really want to get married before the end of the year?"

Pulling her closer, Preston rested his head on the top of her head. "I'd marry you tomorrow if it were possible."

Chandra listened to the strong, steady beats of his heart. "It's not impossible."

He eased back, staring at her with an expression of shock and astonishment freezing his features. "When, Chandra? Let me know the day, time and place and I'll be there."

"We can get married three weeks from now."

Preston massaged her back. "What's happening in three weeks?"

"It will be the Thanksgiving weekend. It's a family holiday, so it shouldn't pose a problem for our families to get together. We're going to have to send out invitations, decide whether we want something simple or formal. And—"

"Slow down, Chandra. You don't have to do anything. We'll hire a wedding planner."

A feeling of unease shuddered over Chandra as if someone were breathing on the back of her neck. She knew for certain that she loved and was in love with Preston Tucker. She also was certain that she wanted to become his wife and the mother of their children, but something from the nightmare continued to chip away at her confidence.

Shaking off the bad vibes as she would an annoying

insect, she forced a smile. "You're right. I'm going to have enough to do when I go back to work."

Dipping his head, Preston placed soft, shivery kisses around her lips, along her jaw and down the column of her neck. "Let me know what you want, and if it's within my power I'll make it happen for you."

Chandra closed her eyes, losing herself in the moment and the man pressed intimately to her heart.

Chandra sat on her bed, cross-legged, the phone cradled between her chin and shoulder. It was her third attempt to procure the services of a wedding planner, and hopefully her last. The first two did not have an opening for the next eight and ten months respectively. Her last hope was Zoë Lang. She'd searched Ms. Lang's Web site and liked what she saw.

"May I make a suggestion, Miss Eaton?"

"Yes, and please call me Chandra."

"Are you opposed to hosting an out-of-state wedding?"

Chandra stopped doodling on the pad resting on her crossed legs. "Where out of the state?"

"Isle of Palms."

She searched her memory as to where she'd heard about Isle of Palms. "Isn't that in South Carolina?"

"Yes, it is. In fact, it's an island off the coast of South Carolina. When you left a message on my voice mail, you said you were willing to assume the expense of lodging out-of-town guests. I've checked with hotels and inns in and around Philadelphia, and most of them are booked up because of the holiday weekend."

"How will Isle of Palms be more convenient?"

"Firstly, Miss…Chandra, it is a summer resort community and after Labor Day many of the vacation properties become available. And secondly, what you'll pay to lodge your guests is considerably lower when compared to a hotel for the Thanksgiving weekend. I'm looking at a listing for an oceanfront villa that will hold a maximum of twenty-two guests for a daily rate of twelve hundred dollars, or a weekly rate of fifty-three hundred. This is far below the average hotel rate of one-fifty a night for three nights. If you were to pay for twenty-two hotel guests for that weekend it would cost you more than twelve thousand dollars."

Chandra jotted down the figures. "I'm going to need more than one villa." Because she wanted a small, intimate wedding, she and Preston had agreed to keep the final count at fifty.

"You're in luck, because I have three properties along the same stretch of beach. There's one with ten bedrooms, ten en suite baths, plus two half baths. There's space for ten cars for a maximum of twenty-six guests."

"How many beds?"

"Six king and four queen beds. The property has three floors, an elevator, high-speed wireless Internet and a boardwalk that leads to a private beach. The total weekly cost for the Thanksgiving week is eighty-three hundred dollars. If you're near a computer I'll send you the link as we speak."

Moving off the bed, Chandra walked out of the bedroom and into the kitchen. Tucked into an alcove was the pantry and a workstation where she'd set up her laptop and printer. "I'm turning on my laptop now." She gave the planner her e-mail address while waiting for her computer to boot; she then logged on to the Internet.

Within minutes she clicked on the link. The seven-thousand-square-foot oceanfront property was exquisite.

It was furnished with a large flat-screen TV and DVD/ VCR combo. All of the second floor bedrooms had deck areas. The kitchen opened out to both the dining and living rooms. Photos of the kitchen revealed stainless steel appliances, gas cooktop, double ovens, subzero refrigerator and granite countertops. She liked the fact that each home came with an initial supply of linens and towels, washer and dryer, cable TV, air conditioning and a starter supply of paper products, detergents and local telephone service. The thing that made her consider holding her wedding on a sea island was the twenty-four-hour security in a gated community.

"I like what I see, Ms. Lang," Chandra told the planner. "I know I'm working within a very tight time frame, but I have to talk to my fiancé before I commit to anything."

"When will you get back to me, Chandra?"

"Either tonight or early tomorrow morning." Preston had called to tell her he had a dinner meeting with a friend, and he would come to her apartment later that evening.

"Whatever you decide, I'll put a rush on the invitations. Right now I need you to fax or e-mail the names and addresses of your guests so the envelopes can be printed."

"I'll e-mail them." Chandra didn't have a fax machine, but Preston did. He had one in the office at his condo and another at his home.

"I'm also going to e-mail my contract. Have your attorney look it over. If you agree with the terms, then send it ASAP."

"Okay. Either I'll speak to you tonight or tomorrow."

"Thank you, Chandra."

"You're welcome, Ms. Lang."

Chandra ended the call, staring at the images on the computer monitor. If anyone would've told her that she was going to marry Preston Tucker after a seven-week whirlwind romance, she would've thought them either certifiably crazy, or at best delusional. Well, the joke was on her, because she *was* going to marry Preston and at present the only question was—where.

She pulled up a map for South Carolina. Preston's mother and sister, who lived in Charleston, were only a few miles from Isle of Palms. East of Charleston and across the Cooper River bridge was the town of Mount Pleasant. Driving east on the bridge would take them to Sullivan's Island and the Isle of Palms.

If she and Preston decided to marry on the sea island, their guests could come days before the ceremony and tour the Carolina low country. For some it could serve as an unforeseen vacation filled with centuries of history waiting to be explored.

The beginnings of a smile softened Chandra's mouth when she stared at the ring on her left hand. She'd reached a decision. She was going to have a low-country wedding.

Preston could not believe the man sitting next to him was his fraternity brother. Clifford Jessup had literally blown up his cell phone when he'd left eleven voice mail messages that he *had* to meet with him. When Preston finally returned the call, he agreed to meet Clifford for dinner. His former agent had asked that he pick him up at a motel in an extremely undesirable part of the city.

"What the hell happened to you?" The question had come out before Preston was able to censor himself. Tall, slender, dark, handsome and always fastidiously groomed, Cliff's suit looked as if he'd slept in it, and with his bearded face and shaggy hair he could've easily passed for a homeless person.

Cliff doffed an imaginary hat. "And, good evening to you, too."

Preston's temper flared. "Either you dial down the sarcastic bull, or get the hell out of my car."

Clifford's face crumbled like an accordion. "Look, P.J., I'm sorry."

"Even if you're not sorry, you're a sorry-looking sight. What's up with you?" Preston's tone had softened considerably.

"Can we go someplace and get something to eat?"

"Sure. But there aren't too many places we can go with you looking like one of Philly's homeless."

Running his hand over the sleeve of his suit jacket, Cliff attempted to smooth out the wrinkles. "It is a little wrinkled."

Preston wanted to tell him it was past wrinkled. Shifting into gear, he backed out of the parking lot of the transient establishment known for its rapid turnover of *guests*.

"There's a diner not too far from here where we can eat."

Slumping down in the leather seat, Cliff closed his eyes. "That sounds good."

Preston gave his passenger a quick glance. He drove down a street where most of the streetlights were out, and probably had been out for weeks. If no one called the city to report the outages, then they probably would remain out indefinitely.

What Preston wanted to know was why Clifford was hanging out in a neighborhood with one of the highest crime rates in the City of Brotherly Love instead of at home with his lovely wife and two beautiful children. He arrived at the diner, maneuvering into the last space between two police cruisers.

They walked into the diner and were shown to a booth in the rear. Cliff requested coffee even before he sat down. Music blared from speakers throughout the twenty-four-hour dining establishment, while flat-screen TVs were turned on, but muted. Preston stared at the closed caption on a channel tuned to CNN.

A waitress brought Cliff his coffee, then took their food order. Preston ordered grilled sole, a baked potato and spinach without reading the extensive menu. Cliff ordered scrambled eggs, grits, bacon, home fries and toast.

Waiting until his former agent downed his second cup of coffee, Preston said, "Why all the 9-1-1 calls?"

Cliff ran a hand over his bearded face. "I need you to talk to Jackie."

Preston leaned forward. "You want me to talk to your wife?" Cliff nodded. "Why?"

"Because I know she'll listen to you, P.J."

"Why would *your* wife listen to me, Cliff?"

"Because she likes you."

"And I like her," Preston countered. He continued to stare at the man whom he had regarded as a brother, a brother that went beyond their belonging to the same fraternity.

"I guess you can say I messed up—big-time—and Jackie told me I couldn't stay in the house."

"Is she talking divorce?"

"No."

"It was a woman." Cliff nodded, while Preston shook his head. He couldn't understand why men cheated on their wives. "Does Jackie know who she is?"

"You could say that."

Preston exhaled an audible breath. "I didn't drive all the way over here to play cat and mouse with you when I could be home with my fiancée."

Cliff closed and opened his eyes and gave his fraternity brother an incredulous stare. "You're getting married?"

Preston smiled for the first time. "Yes. Chandra and I will tie the knot over the Thanksgiving weekend."

"That soon?"

"It's not soon enough for me." He waved a hand. "We're here to talk about you, not me, Brother Jessup."

Cliff smiled. Preston calling him brother was a reminder that although they no longer had a business relationship they were still connected. "Do you remember Kym Hudson?"

Grabbing his forehead, Preston swallowed a savage expletive. He couldn't believe Cliff had mentioned her name. The buxom coed slept her way through their fraternity like a virulent plague. Preston was one of a very few who'd refused to feed her voracious sexual appetite.

"Who could forget Kym the Nymph?" He dropped his hand. "Don't tell me you started up with her again?"

Cliff took a deep swallow of the strong black coffee. "Yeah, and Jackie found out."

"How did she find out?"

"Kym told her."

Preston wanted to reach across the table and grab Cliff by the throat. "You're an asshole! If you're going to cheat on your wife, why do it with someone she knows? I don't blame her for kicking your butt out."

"But—it was only once."

"'It was only once,'" Preston mimicked in falsetto. "You expect Jackie to believe that?"

"But it's true. I only did it because I was curious as to whether she was still *that* good, P.J." Cliff chuckled. "The joke was on me, because she wasn't good at all. All that fake moaning and screaming my name turned my stomach. Meanwhile, I risked losing my wife and children because I couldn't forget some adolescent fantasy."

"I can't talk to Jackie."

"Why not?"

"I'm a writer, not a psychologist or marriage counselor. You have to tell her you want to save your marriage, and if it means going into counseling, then you do it. Meanwhile, if you need a place to live, then you can stay with me at the condo until you get your life back on track."

Cliff stared into his coffee mug. "Thanks, man."

"Did you tell Jackie that you're no longer my agent?"

"No."

"Good. Don't tell her. I'm going to send you and Jackie an invitation to my wedding. Let's hope she'll contact you to ask whether you're attending. Tell her you're going to be my best man."

"Am I going to be your best man?"

"Please shut up and let me finish. As my best man you won't be seated together, but at least you'll get to see her. And, knowing Jackie, I doubt whether she'd make a scene."

Cliff scratched his bearded face. Guilt and anxiety had caused him to lose Preston as a client, but nothing could breach the bond they'd taken as fraternity brothers. "Thanks, Brother Tucker."

Preston affected a stern expression. "The first thing you're going to do when we get back to my place is shave and shower because I don't need an infestation of lice or fleas."

Cliff's teeth shone whitely against his beard. "That's cold, Brother Tucker."

"No, Brother Jessup. That's the deal, or you can continue to live in that turnstile of a cathouse."

Chapter 15

Chandra peered into the adjustable mirror at the back of her wedding gown while the dressmaker tightened the fabric under her armpit, pinning it.

"I'm glad you're getting married in a couple of days, because if not, then I'd have to take your gown in again."

She wanted to tell the talented dressmaker that it was only the second time she'd altered the one-of-a-kind creation. While she was certain that she'd had at least three minor mental breakdowns, her wedding planner was her fairy godmother.

Zoë Lang had arranged for her and Preston to come to Isle of Palms to see the properties where their guests would be housed. She'd mailed off the invitations, monitored the responses by telephone or e-mail, hired local floral and wedding cake designers, DJ and photographer. She and Preston spent two days in

Charleston getting acquainted with her future in-laws. Rose Tucker offered her knowledge of regional lore and cuisine when they sat down to plan the menu and decorations.

Chandra was effusive in her thanks when the wedding planner suggested getting married in the South. After an unusually warm autumn, winter had put in an early appearance in the Northeast. Less than a week into the month of November, Philadelphia had more than eight inches of snowfall.

Many of the guests, looking to take advantage of an impromptu vacation, had elected to arrive early and sign up for the many historic tours in and around Charleston.

"Are you certain it's not too tight?" With the strapless, beaded bodice with an Empire-waist and narrow skirt and bolero-style beaded jacket, Chandra looked as if she'd stepped off the pages of a Jane Austen novel. She had become Josette Fouché in every sense of the word.

Irena Farrow narrowed her eyes. "It's perfect—that is if you don't lose another pound between now and Friday."

"I promise you I won't."

"That's what you said last week."

"I had cramps last week, so all I had was tea and soup."

Irena smiled, her bright blue eyes sparkling like precious jewels. "I used to have cramps so bad that I had to take to my bed for the first two days. But, after I had my Seth they stopped."

Chandra wanted to wait for at least six months before she and Preston started trying for a baby. She'd been hired as a substitute teacher and had to cover a third-grade class for two days since her hire. Substituting fit in perfectly with her current lifestyle. There would be no way she'd be able to plan a wedding with three weeks' notice if she'd had the daily responsibility of her own class.

She felt like a traitor when she told Denise that she would have to give up the co-op once she married Preston. Denise was totally unaffected by the abrupt change in plans because she knew someone looking to rent or sublet a one-bedroom in a nice Philadelphia neighborhood.

Denise had agreed to become a bridal attendant, along with Sabrina and Layla Rice. Belinda, who'd only gained two pounds, was to be her matron of honor. Preston had selected a fraternity brother to be his best man, and Griffin, Myles and his brother-in-law as his groomsmen.

She knew the Eatons and Rices would outnumber the Tuckers two-to-one, but holding the wedding in South Carolina seemed the likely compromise. Barring a tropical storm, Zoë planned a beachfront ceremony and reception under a tent. The ceremony was planned for ten in the morning, followed by brunch. Later that afternoon a six-course dinner would be served. The evening would end with dancing and music supplied by a live band and DJ.

Irena undid the hooks on the back of the gown. "You can get dressed while I alter this. Then you can take it with you."

Chandra's attendants had picked up their dresses the week before. In keeping with an autumnal theme, they would wear slip-style street length dresses in a burnt orange. The color would be repeated in the groomsmen's vests.

She'd borrowed Preston's SUV rather than take a taxi to the dressmaker, while he'd hired a driver to take him to Paoli to meet with Griffin. The aborted meeting with the movie studio executives had been rescheduled with Griffin standing in as Preston's agent.

Irena had sewn the dress and put it in a box filled with tissue paper by the time Chandra had put back on her street clothes. "Take it out of the box and hang it in the garment bag I gave you. Thankfully the wrinkles fall out once it hangs for a few hours." She hugged and kissed Chandra's cheek. "Good luck, darling. You're going to be an exquisite bride."

Chandra returned the hug. "Thank you."

"Don't forget to send me a picture of you and your husband so I can brag that Preston Tucker's wife wore an Irena gown."

"Once they're developed I'll personally bring you one," Chandra promised.

Walking to the rear of the shop, she made her way to the parking lot. Late-morning traffic was light and she made it back to the condo in record time. She parked in the underground garage and took the elevator to the eighteenth floor. Once inside, she took the dress out of the box, storing it in the back of a closet in the smaller of the three second-floor bedrooms.

Skipping down the staircase, Chandra went into the kitchen to gather the ingredients for dinner. She and Preston shared cooking duties, but it was always a special treat whenever he cooked. After brewing a cup of chocolate from the single-cup coffee machine, she made her way to the home/office to use the computer. Denise had begun sending her e-mails every day about things she should do before getting married. Some of them were so hilarious that she laughed until tears rolled down her face.

However, it wasn't Denise's e-mail that garnered her attention, but a draft of *Death's Kiss*. Picking up the unbound pages of the play, she sat on the chaise and began reading.

The hands on her watch had made two revolutions when she turned down the last page. Chandra hadn't realized her hands were shaking uncontrollably until she attempted to gather the pages into a neat pile.

"What are you doing?"

Rising on shaky legs, she saw Preston standing in the doorway. Her shock and rage gave way to a calmness that was scary. A brittle smile hardened her gaze. "I was reading *Death's Kiss*."

He walked into the office. "I didn't want you to read it now. It's only the first draft."

Reaching for the pages, Chandra handed them to him when she wanted to throw them in his face. "Why didn't you tell me, Preston?"

Tapping the pages on the surface of the desk, Preston stacked them neatly, then bound them with a wide rubber band. "Tell you what?"

"Why didn't you tell me you've read my journal?"

Preston affected a sheepish grin. "I was going to tell you."

"When?" she screamed. "When were you going to tell me that you were using me for your own selfish literary pursuits."

His expression changed, becoming a mask of stone. "That's not true, and you know it."

"What I do know is you used my dreams to write your next masterpiece. How do you know I didn't copyright my journals? Then what you've lifted would be deemed plagiarism."

Preston's hands gripped her shoulders, not permitting movement. "Stop it, Chandra."

"I will not stop until I get the hell out of here and away from you."

"No, you're not. You're going to stand here and listen to me."

"I don't want to hear more lies, Preston. I asked you over and over if I could trust you, and you swore I could. Every time we pretended we were Josette and Pascual you must have been laughing at me. Poor little Chandra. She was so taken with the brilliant playwright that she sold herself for a book of dreams. I—"

"Enough!"

She recoiled as if she'd been struck across the face. It was the first time Preston had ever raised his voice to her. Not even her father had raised his voice when speaking to her.

"No, you didn't yell at me."

Preston tightened his hold on Chandra's shoulders when she narrowed her eyes at him. She looked like a cat ready to come at him with fangs and claws.

"I'm sorry, baby. I'd cut off my right arm rather than yell at you."

"Start cutting, because you did," she spat out.

"Chandra, baby, please let me say something." He felt her shoulders relax. Gathering her to his chest, he pressed a kiss to her forehead. "I was going to tell you once the play was sent to the Library of Congress for a copyright." He released her, walked over to the desk and returned with a single sheet of paper and handed it to her.

Chandra felt her knees buckle as she inched over

to sit on the chaise. She read what he'd typed three times before the realization hit her: A Play in Three Acts written by C. E. and P. J. Tucker. He'd included her as the coauthor of *Death's Kiss*.

"Why did you put my name first?" she whispered.

Going to a knee, Preston cradled the back of her head. "Don't you know you come first in my life? I love you, baby. I'd love you even if I never read a word in your journal."

"But you did read it and didn't tell me."

"I didn't want to embarrass you, Chandra, because you'd have to explain if you'd slept with the man in your dreams or if he was an imaginary person you'd conjured up to assuage your sexual frustration."

Chandra demurely lowered her eyes. "It was the latter."

"All I can say is you have a helluva imagination."

She pressed her forehead to his. "What you read is tame. I have three other volumes and most of them are X-rated."

"What I read was X-rated."

"Then double and triple X-rated."

"Dam-n-n. Don't tell me I'm marrying a freak!"

Chandra swatted at him, but missed his head when he ducked. "I'll freak you."

Easing her off the chaise, Preston pressed her down to the floor. "I just happen to like freaks. The freakier the better."

She smiled up at the man she didn't want to trust, and the one with whom she'd fallen inexorably in love. "I'm kind of partial to freaks, too. What do you say we get our freak on before we fly down to Isle of Palms tomorrow."

Chandra would stay in the villa with eighteen other

Eatons and Rices. Preston would live in another villa a thousand feet away with his close friends and relatives. A third villa would accommodate an overflow of friends and family.

She and Preston would remain on the island until Sunday afternoon when they'd fly down to St. Barts for a two-week honeymoon before returning to Philadelphia.

"I'm game if you are," Preston agreed, "but only if you're on top."

"Let's do it, P.J."

Pushing to his feet, Preston swept Chandra off the floor, carried her out of the office and up the staircase to the master bedroom. He took his time undressing her, then himself. There was no need to rush because they had the rest of their lives to live out their sweet dreams.

The weather on Isle of Palms was perfect for an outdoor wedding. A cooling breeze off the river offset the heat of the sun on the bared skin of those who'd come as couples and in groups all week to the sea island to relax and take in the history of the low country.

Pumpkins, stalks of corn and decorative sweetgrass baskets lined the beach as bridesmaids and groomsmen lined the double staircase leading to the two story villa flanked by palmetto trees.

Preston Tucker stood at the foot of the staircases. He was waiting for Dr. Dwight Eaton to escort his daughter through the open French doors. The familiar strains of the "Wedding March" caught everyone's attention, and those sitting under the tent stood up. A lump formed in his throat, he finding it difficult to swallow.

Carrying a bouquet of yellow chrysanthemums,

orange blossoms, yellow and orange sunflowers, Chandra carefully navigated the orange runner, the toes of her white satin ballet-type slippers peeking from under the hem of her gown. A light breeze lifted the chapel veil attached to the crown of her head with a jeweled comb.

A minister stood ready to begin officiating. "Who gives this woman in this most sacred rite of matrimony?"

Dwight Eaton appeared to have grown an inch when he pulled back his shoulders. "I do."

It was the second time within four months that he would give away a daughter in marriage, and the third in which he'd witnessed the wedding of his children. All of his surviving children were married, and he and Roberta were looking forward to many more grandchildren.

Chandra smiled at her father. "I love you, Daddy."

He winked at her. "Be happy, baby girl."

She nodded. "I will."

The wedding party descended the staircases to stand opposite one another alongside the carpet when Dwight placed Chandra's hand on Preston's outstretched one.

Chandra focused on the orange blossom boutonniere rather than his face because she didn't want to cry and ruin her makeup. Earlier that morning he'd sent Clifford Jessup to give her a gift. When she'd unwrapped the small package it was to find a pair Cartier South Sea pearls with yellow oval diamonds. The attached card read:

To be worn on special occasions—weddings, births and award ceremonies. Love always, Pascual.

She glanced up through her lashes to see him staring

at her lobes. She'd worn the earrings. A smile trembled over her lips. "I will love you forever."

Preston lowered his head, lightly touching her mouth with his. "Thank you, darling."

The minister cleared his throat as a ripple of laughter came from the assembled. "The groom usually kisses his bride *after* I pronounce them husband and wife."

"Sorry about that."

The minister straightened his tie under his black robe. "Let's get started, so you can get to kiss your wife instead of your bride."

"I'm ready," Preston said softly.

And he was ready to love and live out all the sweet dreams his wife recorded in her journals.

An exchange of vows, followed by an exchange of rings and they were now husband and wife.

When Chandra Eaton came home she'd planned to stay. What she hadn't planned on was becoming Mrs. Chandra Eaton-Tucker, wife of celebrated playwright Preston Tucker.

Life was not only good.

It was sweet.